TERMINAL BOREDOM

TERMINAL BOREDOM

Stories

Izumi Suzuki

Translated by Polly Barton, Sam Bett,
David Boyd, Daniel Joseph,
Aiko Masubuchi, and Helen O'Horan

VERSO
London • New York

With support from the Japan Foundation

JAPANFOUNDATION

First published by Verso 2021
The stories here appeared originally in Japanese in *Keiyaku: Suzuki Izumi Sf Zenshū*
(Covenant: The Complete Science Fiction of Suzuki Izumi), by Suzuki Izumi
Collection copyright © 2014 by Suzuki Azusa
Originally published in Japan by BUNYU-SHA Inc.
English translation rights arranged with BUNYU-SHA Inc.
through The Sakai Agency
Translation of 'Women and Women' and 'Terminal Boredom' © Daniel Joseph 2021
Translation of 'You May Dream' © David Boyd 2021
Translation of 'Night Picnic' © Sam Bett 2021
Translation of 'That Old Seaside Club' © Helen O'Horan 2021
Translation of 'Smoke Gets in Your Eyes' © Aiko Masubuchi 2021
Translation of 'Forgotten' © Polly Barton 2021
All rights reserved
The moral rights of the author have been asserted

5 7 9 10 8 6

Verso
UK: 6 Meard Street, London W1F 0EG
US: 20 Jay Street, Suite 1010, Brooklyn, NY 11201
versobooks.com

Verso is the imprint of New Left Books

ISBN-13: 978-1-78873-988-7
ISBN-13: 978-1-78873-989-4 (UK EBK)
ISBN-13: 978-1-78873-990-0 (US EBK)

British Library Cataloguing in Publication Data
A catalogue record for this book is available from the British Library

Library of Congress Cataloging-in-Publication Data

Names: Suzuki, Izumi, 1949–1986, author. | Barton, Polly (Translator),
translator. | Bett, Sam, 1986–, translator. | Boyd, David (David G.),
translator. | Joseph, Daniel (Translator), translator. | Masubuchi,
Aiko, translator. | O'Horan, Helen, translator.
Title: Terminal boredom : stories / Izumi Suzuki, translated by Polly
Barton, Sam Bett, David Boyd, Daniel Joseph, Aiko Masubuchi, and Helen
O'Horan.
Description: London ; New York : Verso, 2021. | Summary: 'Born from the
obsessive and highly idiosyncratic mind of a cult figure of the Japanese
underground, these stories borrow themes and subjects familiar to
readers of Philip K. Dick and fuses them with a conflicted, tortured,
and intense imagination' – Provided by publisher.
Identifiers: LCCN 2020047575 (print) | LCCN 2020047576 (ebook) | ISBN
9781788739887 (paperback) | ISBN 9781788739900 (ebk)
Subjects: LCSH: Suzuki, Izumi, 1949–1986 – Translations into English. |
LCGFT: Short stories.
Classification: LCC PL861.U9265 A2 2021 (print) | LCC PL861.U9265 (ebook)
| DDC 895.63/5 – dc23
LC record available at https://lccn.loc.gov/2020047575
LC ebook record available at https://lccn.loc.gov/2020047576

Typeset in Electra by Hewer Text UK Ltd, Edinburgh
Printed and bound by CPI Group (UK) Ltd, Croydon CR0 4YY

CONTENTS

WOMEN AND WOMEN

This morning a boy passed by my house.

When I told my sister Asako about it, she just said, 'Dummy, you know there aren't any boys around here.'

And she was right.

Long ago, the Earth was peopled only by women. They lived in peace until one day a certain woman gave birth to a child unlike any that had come before: its body was misshapen, it was rough and careless in everything it did, and it made a great deal of trouble for everyone before it produced a few offspring and then died. Such was the advent of man. From there, the number of men increased steadily. It was they who invented war and its requisite implements. Worse still, they began to toy with notions like revolution, work, and art, wasting their energy on all manner of abstract pursuits. And they even had the audacity to claim that this, *this* was the greatest character-istic of mankind – this zealous pursuit of adventure, romance, all things that were utterly useless in everyday life. Though men were adults they were children, seemingly complex but as simple as could be; they were utterly unmanageable creatures.

Women had something as well, something called 'love', but this was much more concrete. It was putting up with a crying baby, changing its diapers even though you were exhausted. It was sharing any food you found with the weak little beings in your care. But not with outsiders. Because if you did that, you and your bloodline would not survive.

As the number of men increased, the women had to keep a close eye on each and every one of them. This was a truly onerous task, but most women seemed to have the knack for it. They had to safeguard home and family.

With the passage of many long years, men came to dominate society through violence and cunning, and thereafter they made nothing but war. They seemed to find their raison d'être in conflicts both great and small. War found its way even into everyday life, and so were born 'traffic wars' and 'admissions wars'. Such terms became so common that the word 'war' lost all meaning. This deplorable situation was of course the men's fault. And, when the traffic snarls and college entrance competition got so bad that people could hardly bear it, they replaced the word 'war' with 'hell', coining phrases like 'traffic hell' and 'exam hell'.

Factories continued to operate, and the age resounded with hymns of progress and harmony. But then, in the latter half of the twentieth century, a strange thing happened: the male birth rate began to decline. This was apparently due to something called pollution. The men who invented the steam engine probably never expected to set in motion events that would bring an end to their own kind.

In any case, men became scarce. For some reason women had developed the habit of each finding a particular man to love, so they were terribly sad about this. Nevertheless, the number of men continued to dwindle.

Nowadays, you'll never even lay eyes on one unless you visit the Gender Exclusion Terminal Occupancy Zone.

'You sure you weren't just seeing things?'

Asako poured some tea. My confidence evaporated in the face of her question.

'Maybe. But afterwards I looked it up in a book, and the clothes he was wearing were a lot like the ones boys wore towards the end of the twentieth century. His hair was short, and he was wearing trousers.'

'Same goes for me.'

Asako's hair was indeed cropped short, and she had on a pair of light cotton bell-bottoms.

'I mean, sure, but his trousers were a lot tighter and not so wide at the bottom. And his chest was flat as a board.'

'There are women like that too, you know.'

'His whole vibe was different. He was solidly built and tall, with a spring in his step. There was something . . . intense about him.'

'Wow. Well, looks like you've got all the answers, never mind the fact that you've never even seen a man before. The year I graduated high school we went on a field trip to the Occupancy Zone, but men turned out to be nothing like I expected. They were scraggly and smelled funny, and they all gave me the creeps. Maybe it's because they're stuck in that place, but they all seemed so lazy. You'll understand when you go and see them. They're awful. But you said you looked it up in a book. Where did you see a book like that?'

The publication of material concerning men is strictly prohibited.

'A friend's house.'

'Well, how'd it get there?'

'I guess her mother works for the Information Bureau. My friend doesn't really know either. She opened the door to the study with a hairpin and said I could read any book I wanted.'

'Such a little hoodlum.'

'There were lots of films, too.'

'If that got out, it would mean real trouble. Yūko, I know you don't really understand, but that kind of thing could throw society into chaos. I want you to remember this: order is the most important thing. Abiding by the rules. If we all do that, humanity can avoid destruction.'

She gave this lecture gently, like a proper big sister.

I poured some milk into my tea. 'By humanity, you mean women?'

'Of course. Didn't you learn that in school?'

'Yeah.'

'Well, there you go.'

'And men?'

'Men are an offshoot of humanity as well, but they're a deviant strain. They're freaks.'

'But there was a time when they flourished, wasn't there?'

They don't teach us much about that in school. You only learn about such taboo subjects through whispered conversations among friends. Two or three years back, someone secretly

4

published a pamphlet called *On Men*, and a friend showed it to me. Eventually the police cracked down and seized all the copies. The culprits were quickly caught and put in a detention facility.

The news posters branded it a dangerous publication because it 'stimulated curiosity'.

My grandmother told me that when she was young they used to deliver the newspaper door to door each morning, and the transportation network extended to every corner of the country. Even now you can go see the massive concrete pillars that used to hold up the highways. You never know when they might collapse, though, so it's dangerous to get too close. It was around the same time resources started to become scarce and they scaled back production in the factories that the number of men also started to decrease. We were taught that it was the men who had created that horrifying culture. By the end, they had used up almost all of the oil; the deposits are all but depleted now, so we rely almost entirely on the heat of the sun. Women have been left carefully husbanding the scant resources of a planet stripped bare by men.

Apparently back then there was also something called a TV in every home. I can't even imagine – all kinds of programmes coming at you from morning till night, at the twist of a knob. And all for free! I guess something called NHK collected money for it, but towards the end nobody paid anymore. TV was one of women's greatest pleasures. Grandma says when she was a kid she used to watch it every day. Back then girls and boys alike were immersed in exam hell, but her mother didn't give her any grief about school. Grandma wanted to be a singer. She told me so. Apparently at that time, these singers would appear on TV constantly. And since just about everyone watched TV, they were famous, and if you were famous, throngs of people would come to your concerts. I don't really believe the part about everybody watching TV, though. Grandma also told me it was really sad when the TV stations went under and men weren't around as much anymore.

'Stop talking nonsense and go to bed already . . . It's eight o'clock, the electricity's about to get shut off.'

And sure enough, just as my sister said this, the already dim bulb went dark. In its wake, the moonlight lay in stripes across the tabletop.

'Look, the moon's so big and red,' Asako pointed. 'Look where it is.'

We sat together, sipping the last of our tea as we gazed out at the moon hanging low in the sky, its unsettling colour giving it a bloated, spongy look.

'I wonder what Mum's doing now.'

This was something we were never supposed to talk about. But my sister didn't reprimand me. In fact, she tried to console me.

'We'll see her again next month.'

'Yeah.'

But our monthly meetings only lasted for ten minutes or so. And there was always a guard present, so we could never say what we were actually thinking. Lately Mother had been getting weepy every time we had to say goodbye.

'Why *did* they put her in a detention centre?'

'Because she broke the law,' Asako answered automatically. But the truth was, she didn't know much about the circumstances of her arrest. One day some strangers showed up out of the blue and just took our mother away. Asako was four or five at the time, and she remembers it pretty well considering.

'According to Grandma, she was harbouring a dangerous individual.' Her tone started to falter.

'What happened to that person?'

'Arrested, of course, and most likely sent away someplace else. But it's blessing enough that we get to see Mum face to face, since I'm pretty sure it was the secret police who took her away.'

'Is there really such a thing?'

'I think so . . . This is all just a guess, though, and you mustn't tell anyone.'

'I know that.'

'I think they might be connected to the Information Bureau somehow, but keep that just between ourselves as well.'

'Okay, I get it already.'

'As far as anyone knows, our mother is dead. If this got out, it could upset the social order.'

'Okay.'

I think my sister's a little too high-strung. Maybe because Mum was taken away when she was so little.

'I wouldn't be able to go to work anymore, either.'

Asako's such a nag. I lit a candle. It was a cheap, smelly thing, but it was better than what most of our neighbours used: wicks dipped in animal fat. They were smoky and smelled horrible. We decided not to be stingy when it comes to light.

'I'm going to bed. I'll do the dishes in the morning.' I stood up to leave.

'It's fine, I'll wash them tonight,' my sister replied. 'The stairs are dark, why don't you take the candle with you.'

'I'm used to it.'

I paused at the foot of the stairs. Here, too, moonlight was streaming in through the window. I had been up since early that morning and now I was exhausted.

I'd woken up around four a.m., unable to stand the sweltering heat. The little window in my bedroom was shut, so I went over and opened it up wide. That's when I saw the boy, going by on the road below. No one should be out and about at that hour, so I studied him carefully.

In my room on the second floor, I opened my diary in the small patch of moonlight. The diary was a present from Grandma for my sixteenth birthday; I'd been writing in it for two years now.

I intended to write about what had happened that morning, but my sister's words had shaken my confidence. My eyesight's really good, but it's not going to stay that way if I keep on writing by moonlight every night. Since I'd decided not to tell anyone else about the boy, I wouldn't mention it in my diary either. I wrote the date, paused, and then thought for a minute.

Today our teacher took us to the theatre. They had the marquee lights on even during the daytime, and I was shocked at how bright it was. I've never been somewhere so lively, and so many things were new to me. Maki said, 'I hear sometimes they put men on stage here. They do something called boxing.' And Rei said, 'Not here, they don't. That happens at a gymnasium or

8

something.' Then the teacher walked by, so we all clammed up
and went inside. The lighting on the inside was bright too, it was
so pretty. On the way back we rode in a horse-drawn carriage.

Asako says that horse-drawn carriages are on the way out
too. Come to think of it, I haven't seen as many lately. Then
again, it's a real luxury just to ride in anything, whether it's
a horse-drawn carriage or the more common pollution-free
automobiles. If it's not going to take more than an hour or so,
most people just walk. I was literally bursting with joy that I'd
gotten to ride in a carriage, so I had to put it in my diary. Asako
works at an energy research facility. She says they're gradually
implementing the use of uranium and plutonium. And solar
technology is getting better and better all the time. But she also
said something disturbing about how 'the sun is sort of like a
big cluster of hydrogen bombs'.

I opened the window and looked down at the road below,
but of course there was no one there.

Had my eyes been playing tricks on me that morning after
all?

I got into bed.

The zelkovas were rustling outside.

I heard the stairs creak.

'Are you asleep?' my sister asked from the other side of my
door.

'Uhh . . .'

My non-committal reply came out sounding like a moan.

'You understand, right? Not to tell anyone what you told
me.' Asako lowered her voice even further.

'Yeah, I understand,' I answered in a drowsy voice.

'You can't go around telling people you saw a boy.'

Enough already.

'Don't worry about it.'

I could picture Asako standing at the head of the stairs holding the candle. She was silent for a while. I guess she must've been mulling something over. Or maybe it was supposed to be one of those demonstrative silences.

'. . . Right. Okay, good night then.'

She finally went to her room.

'Night,' I muttered curtly (though I don't think she heard me) and pulled the covers up to my chest. I always lie awake in bed for two or three hours before I fall asleep. But this time I felt like I could drift off right away.

When I awoke, it was still dark.

I couldn't tell what time it was. The clock's in the living room, and it was too much of a pain to go check, so I just lay there.

I tried to reconnect the fragments of my dreams but without much success. And I felt well-rested enough that there was no point trying to go back to sleep. I wasn't the slightest bit tired.

I got up and put my clothes on in the dark.

Opening the desk drawer, I took out a cigarette I had filched from my sister's room. She smokes herself, so I wasn't worried about the smell giving me away. And Grandma almost never comes upstairs.

I lit the cigarette and took a drag, and within a few seconds I felt like all the blood was ebbing away from my body. It was as if all the air inside my head had been let out. I started to feel dizzy, so I sat down. My fingertips felt cold.

In that moment the music from the previous afternoon's performance came back to me. It was a new musical, a love story about a heroine named Sappo or Sappho or something, and everyone had been crazy about the actor playing her. Most of the students raved about how gorgeous she was, and it was clear everyone had a huge crush on her. I felt the same way, but I kept my mouth shut. It rubbed me the wrong way – I was finally at the age to start dating, but the most excitement I'd had in that department was an anonymous love letter or two.

During the intermission we went to the lobby to buy some sweets. There were lots of steady couples standing around together. The teacher was there so no one was necking or anything, but it was still aggravating.

Neither Maki nor Rei has a special someone either, so the three of us buddied up and ate some biscuits together. We probably seemed like the three class dogs.

'That actress is gorgeous, huh? I'd love to be with someone like that!' The area around Rei's eyes had gone a pale peach colour. What's got you so hot and bothered, I thought to myself.

'What would you do if you were?' asked Maki.

'I'd whip up a nice lunch every day for her to take to work.'

'Pssh, that's ridiculous. Nothing good can come of having a crush on someone like that. She'd definitely cheat on you. She probably has little pillow queens all over town.'

You can use that kind of vulgar slang only among friends. There were rumours that Maki's a top, not that she's popular at all. One time she showed me one of her love letters, but

11

everything she'd written was so crude that I rewrote it for her. She ended up sending the one she'd come up with on her own, though, which is maybe why she got her heart broken yet again. The younger girl she was hot for ran off with some good-for-nothing who was a lot older.

Maki was determined to show her by 'becoming a hoodlum', but other than taking up smoking (she gives me cigarettes occasionally, so I'm not complaining), she's just as unpopular as ever.

Cigarettes are a real luxury item, and almost nowhere sells them. They have a terribly acrid taste and the packages look filthy, but you'd be lucky to get a pack for two kilos of rice.

'Fuck actresses. They're the enemy.' Maki was getting herself worked up.

Graduation was coming up soon, so everyone had been out of sorts lately. September meant the end of school.

The kids from the Cinema Studies Club had gone to a secret screening recently, and it turned into a big thing. The newspaper even carried the story, and they all ended up getting expelled.

They'd watched an old movie from before the revision of the penal code. It was called *American Graffiti* or something, and not only does it feature lots of men, it doesn't depict them the way the authorities think a movie should. The world was a really terrible place before it got to be like it is now, but apparently they don't want anybody seeing this movie because it presents that time in an attractive light. Though it wasn't the students themselves who'd taken it from the Cultural Centre, of course.

Men sometimes still appear in movies but only as adults. And even though they don't show anything below the neck, no one under the age of eighteen is allowed to see them.

By the time I had finished leisurely smoking the precious cigarette, the world outside my window had begun making its way toward dawn.

I carried the chair over to the window and sat looking out.

If he hadn't been a hallucination, there was always the chance that the boy might pass this way again. I waited with my elbows propped on the windowsill, but he never showed. Did he know I'd seen him? He might be on the run from the Occupancy Zone, in which case, did I need to warn him? It was one thing for me to spot him, but if anyone else did they'd report it to the police, no question.

With one eye still focused on the road outside, I returned to my desk.

'What's your name? Why are you here? I won't tell anyone (I promise), so please answer. I want to be friends.'

I wrote this on a scrap of paper torn from my notebook and folded it up long and thin, then wrapped it around the neck of a ceramic rabbit and tied a ribbon over it to hold it in place. I'd bought the ribbon the previous Sunday when my sister and I went to the high street. It was dark blue, with gold lamé. It felt a little wasteful since I'd never even worn it once, but oh well.

Returning to the window with the figure of the rabbit in my hands, I continued my vigil. What if he couldn't read? Going by what my sister had said, it didn't sound like there were schools or anything in the GETO.

Eventually a figure emerged from the trees – the same person as yesterday. He didn't seem to be in any particular hurry, but he'd have been trying not to draw attention to himself, so who knows.

I dropped the rabbit out the window so it landed right at his feet, and he looked up. I smiled to put him at ease, and then grabbed a light cotton handkerchief that was sitting nearby and dropped it down as well.

I had embroidered the handkerchief myself, and it had taken three whole days. My sister hates handicrafts, so I'd gotten Grandma to teach me.

The boy (if that's what he was) seemed startled at first and stared suspiciously up at my grinning face. His apparent fearlessness thrilled me.

He picked up the rabbit and gave me a questioning look. I nodded, and then moved away from the window so as not to scare him. Not that he seemed in the least bit frightened.

I lay on my bed and folded my arms under my head. I just spaced out for a while, not thinking about anything in particular, during which time a clear impression of the person passing below the window took hold in my mind.

I went downstairs and looked for something to eat, but there was nothing in the cabinets other than some bread and tinned goods. Not many households have refrigerators. Grandma says that in her day they were everywhere.

Has the world taken a step backward? Whenever I ask that question, my sister gets angry. 'Looking at the world through the lens of progress is how the rivers and oceans ended up polluted,' she says. But that's not what I mean. Though one time she also said, 'Time passes, the planet has its many histories, and things decline. That's all there is to it.'

They say if you go to London or New York nowadays, it's just the same as here. Though it's incredibly difficult to leave the country in the first place. If you ever managed it, you'd be a celebrity anywhere you went. You'd be in all the newspapers (which are only distributed to schools and workplaces and other public facilities), and you'd probably even be on the radio. There are only two radio stations, and they broadcast from seven to ten in the morning and five till eight at night. It's my dream to see other countries, but it'll probably never come true.

I rested my elbows on the kitchen table and munched on a piece of bread that tasted like boiled roots. I'd have loved to eat something that actually tasted good. But our household gets by on my sister's income alone. Since there's a criminal in our family, we aren't eligible for public assistance. Grandma does a little piecework on the side, but that barely brings in anything. We get by thanks to the free meals they give out at school and work. I spread some margarine on the bread. The hands of the clock pointed to 5:17. The person had passed under my window just after four.

Bread in hand, I put on my sandals and went outside. I inspected the area under my window – the ceramic rabbit and handkerchief were both gone. He'd accepted my gifts. How disappointed I would've been if they were still there!

I finished the bread where I stood, in the flood of morning sunlight.

~

'Yūko, you sleepwalking or something? What are you doing with your bookbag? There's no class today,' Maki reminded me. 'You've been kind of weird lately. Did you find a special someone?'

Rei was chewing on her pencil.

'Umm, well . . . something like that,' I replied vaguely. It'd been two weeks. I'd been waking up super early every day and keeping watch from my window at dawn. He comes by about once every three days. We still haven't spoken. We just wave to each other.

'Who is it?' Maki raised her eyebrows.

'It's a s-s-secret.' I pulled a suggestive expression. I tend to only play things up like that when there's nothing actually going on, and so they both lost interest immediately.

'Rei's been writing letters to that actress every single day, sending her flowers even. What a moron, right?' Maki said.

'And?'

'And here's the thing. She got a response, but now she doesn't know what to do.'

Rei continued wretchedly chewing her pencil.

'She was writing *I want to see you, I want to see you*, and going to her house every morning to deliver her letter, then one morning they ran into each other when the actress was coming home from a long night out. And she said, "You're cute" or something or took her hand . . .' Maki turned to look at Rei, who frowned. 'The truth is she did more than that, though, didn't she? Didn't she?' Maki tickled Rei's neck. Rei flinched and knocked her hand away.

'So what'd she say?' I asked dutifully. '*I'd like to see you again* or something?' I didn't think that actress was even the slightest bit attractive anymore. I hadn't since that mystery person first showed up outside my window. I'd had my share of crushes on actresses and stars before, and I'd always looked forward to our semi-annual trips to the theatre, saving up my basically non-existent pocket money in advance.

'That's the thing. What she said was, *I want to be with you,*' Rei answered gloomily. Though she was definitely happy about it.

'Like, live together?' It was a tedious topic. But I tried to play along anyway.

'*I'll inform the office,*' she told me. '*We'll have a ceremony, and I want to have kids.*'

'Wow, no shit?'

Once you're above a certain age, if you decide you want kids, you go to the hospital. Even if you're unmarried, it's fine as long as you can raise them. They probably inject you with some medicine or something.

'You're not going to look for a job?'

'I'm not cut out for it,' Rei replied shamelessly. 'Even if this doesn't work out, I'll just find an arranged marriage.' Rei has a pretty face and pale skin, giving her good reason to be confident of finding someone to support her. Long ago, it was normal for the men to work while the women took care of the household chores, and that arrangement hasn't really changed – all that's new is that it's the more masculine woman who goes to work, while the more feminine partner takes care of the sundry other tasks at home.

The bell rang.

'What're we doing today?' I asked Maki.

'Field trip to the GETO,' she replied, a disgusted look on her face. 'Gross, right? Why would anyone want to go see that? But it'll be educational at least, so I guess I'm not gonna not go.'

Women live with other women. The strange thing is, one of them always does her best to emulate what we're told masculinity was like in the old days. Maybe that's what she meant by 'educational'. Not that a bunch of young girls' notion of masculinity is worth much.

The bus came to a stop outside the GETO, on the outskirts of town.

'Looks like an ancient Roman coliseum, huh?' said Maki. 'From the outside, anyway.'

With its towering walls, the place looked like an impregnable fortress to me.

'I keep expecting Davy Crockett to pop out.'

'Who's that?' Rei could barely keep her eyes open.

'From the Alamo,' I replied.

'Oh, history from *before*.' She sounded totally disinterested.

'Okay, everyone, time to get off the bus. Form two lines,' the teacher shouted.

We filed down a narrow stairwell that led underground. Muffled giggles and secret conversations echoed off the cement walls.

'Why's it underground?'

'They have a vegetable garden on the surface.'

We came to a guardroom where two armed guards sat side by side smoking cigarettes. The grey uniform suited the one on the left to a tee, but the other had enormous breasts and it looked odd on her.

Our teacher showed the field trip permit at the window. The guards took a headcount and made a cursory survey of our faces as if that might flush out any guerrillas lurking in our midst. If they're so worried, why not stop having these field trips in the first place? Though anyone who missed this opportunity would most likely never discover what sort of thing a male really is.

One of the guards unlocked the iron doors. The students filed through, gabbling excitedly.

'Are there still boys being born?'

'Of course there are,' answered Maki. 'You're so ignorant.'

'Then why don't you ever see them in town? You only ever see girl babies in prams.'

'Because boy children are incredibly rare. The pollution had genetic effects too, you know.'

'Still.'

'Plus, when a boy child *is* born, they take him away immediately. I guess when a boy is born they announce it as a still-birth. That way everybody can breathe easier. But it's like the whole thing gets hushed up. I mean, being born a boy is like a deformity, you've got no choice but to accept it.'

Maki really knows a lot.

There were fluorescent lights installed in the ceiling of the long underground passage. The complex probably had its own electrical generator. They have them in hospitals and big hotels, after all. The facility was much larger than it had seemed from the outside.

At the end of the passageway there was another guardroom and two more guards, plus someone who seemed like a guide, all looking totally bored.

One of the guards was scratching her head as she read a book, raining dandruff down onto the open pages. A faint beard emphasized her jawline, probably the result of some hormonal imbalance, but she also had an ample chest. It made me uncomfortable. Who knows, she might've even been given male hormones at the hospital.

At the time I couldn't help but feel kind of repulsed on seeing a woman with a crew cut, wearing trousers, her breasts bound. I'd been feeling that way ever since I first encountered the boy I gave the ceramic rabbit to. There was something refreshing, invigorating about him. Now when I see these women who try to emulate the masculinity of the old days without really knowing anything about it, I feel weird, like I can't breathe. Fortunately, there aren't so many these days. 'That's an old trend. Things are cooler now. We're all the same sex, so what's the point of trying to maintain a gendered division of labour?' I'm pretty sure Rei said something like that, anyway.

There was an iron door here as well. The guard opened it and the guide stepped through. 'Okay, we'll begin with the kitchen.'

The place seemed huge inside, maybe even bigger below ground than the walled-off area up above. You could tell just from the size of the hallways and rooms. Who knows, the underground part might even be three or four levels deep!

They only show students a small part of it, I imagine.

'This place is like an enormous hospital,' the guide told us. 'Here we see to the needs of those poor souls unfortunate enough to be born male.'

The kitchen was cavernous and deserted. Huge pots and ladles lined the walls.

'It's lunchtime right now, so everyone's in the dining hall.'

There was nothing interesting to see. It was like exploring an empty cruise ship, though pitifully grimy in comparison. It must be an old facility, I guessed, to be so shabby.

'And this is where they sleep. There are a number of rooms like this.'

The beds stood in ranks. In one lay a man with a face like a rat.

'Hey, you there, what's wrong with you?'

A murmur passed among the students as the guide addressed him, everyone whispering their impressions to one another.

'My stomach hurts,' whimpered the man (of indeterminate age, though there was nothing youthful about him). Then, pretending to avert his eyes, he flicked a series of sidelong glances our way.

'What about the other one, with the sprained ankle?' inquired the guide.

'Oh, B-0372? He went to the refectory on crutches.'

They don't even have names!

That's because they're not considered human. That is, they *aren't* human. But even cats and dogs get names . . . Not to mention that females still need male cooperation to have children.

I don't know too much about it, but apparently males are raised in these facilities in order to collect some kind of secretion they produce. Beyond that, I'm pretty much in the dark.

'Like keeping honeybees?' I asked Maki, always an authority on such matters.

'Hmm, no, not quite. Though the sexual morphology of our society is maybe similar. Except that with honeybees, there's only one queen.'

'And we're all queens,' Rei cut in, bursting into giggles.

'We all have the potential to be, anyway,' I replied, showing off some meagre wisdom of my own. 'Since all you have to do to have a baby is go to the hospital. And those who don't want to, don't have to. That's how we took care of the population problem.'

There was nothing charming or interesting about the rat-faced man, and the students all blithely returned to their idle chatter. But for me it had been a real shock.

That feeling stayed with me for the rest of the trip. The thing is, the males in that place were nothing at all like the boy who passed by my house on those early mornings. They didn't even seem like the same species. Even though I'd never exchanged a word with the boy, I was certain that he wasn't female. But no matter how much I searched for the same aura among the males in that place, it was nowhere to be found.

They seemed to be uniformly apathetic and timid, their vacant expressions suggesting low intelligence.

The other students were getting bored and antsy. The orderly line began to fall apart, and people started horsing around.

'Quiet, everyone, quiet!'

Our teacher was sweating bullets, but the guide was beaming.

'How nice it is to be in the presence of so many young women for the first time in what feels like forever. You're all so wonderfully lively. Working here isn't very rewarding, you know. No matter what we do for them, we get no gratitude, and when someone does say thank you, they don't really mean it. The men are all infected with a terrible indifference. Nothing to be done about it, though, that's just how men are.'

Hang on. That doesn't seem right. I'm pretty sure if I was locked up in a place like that for my whole life and never allowed to leave, I'd end up apathetic too.

Then, when the tour was over and we were about leave, something happened.

Mealtime had ended by the time we passed by the refectory and there was no sign of anyone inside, but suddenly a man leapt out and threw his arms around one of the students. She shrieked, and our teacher and the guide grabbed hold of the man and pulled him off her right away.

The guide began reprimanding the man and pressed a buzzer. Three guards charged up and seized him.

The student stood there startled, but she didn't faint or anything.

'My apologies, young lady, I'm glad you're alright. This isn't the first time that man has done something like this. He's not mentally ill, but there's clearly something wrong with him. Although this is the first time he's attacked a student . . . How many times will he have to do this sort of thing before he's satisfied, I wonder.'

Deciding perhaps that it would be inappropriate to say more, the guide left it at that.

'They're so dangerous,' remarked our teacher.

I couldn't for the life of me figure out why she thought that. But, more important, I couldn't understand why that man attacked a student. If he resented the world outside the GETO, you'd think he would've used a weapon, a knife or a meat cleaver or something. I couldn't quite figure out what had motivated him to attack her, to wrap his arms around her the way he did.

Maybe our teacher didn't know either.

In the bus on the way back, the students were all saying, 'That wasn't what I was hoping for at all,' and so on. At school right now, manga from *before* is really trendy. Most of the movies and books from *before* are banned, but what used to be called 'girl's manga' is still permitted. The males who appear in it are quite young for the most part, and they're all extremely charming. Most of the girls who imitate men nowadays use these characters as their point of reference. They're all convinced that's what men are like.

The heroines of these stories typically fall in love with skinny guys. Big fat men do appear sometimes, but only as comic relief; they're never the protagonist. The love interests have long spindly arms and legs and delicate features, and they're detached or sweet or naïve. You never really see passionate men in these comics. According to Rei, the actresses who get super popular on account of their manliness are all 'extremely passionate'.

Anyway, it was because all these schoolgirls had been reading manga from *before* that they were so disappointed by the men they saw on the field trip.

24

'They gave me the creeps.' This was Rei.

'Not even one of them was attractive at all. None of them had white hands or long fingers or anything!' They'd all been hoping for beautiful men.

'It was like a zoo.'

'Not really, but it sure was like they were a different species or something.'

'Why on earth did people marry men *before*?'

'Maybe because the men *before* were like the ones in manga?'

'They've gone downhill, no question about it.'

'Or maybe the manga from *before* was just pure fantasy. Maybe the actual men weren't like that at all, maybe they were stronger. That's what my great aunt told me, anyway, and she used to live with a man. She said that most men used to be way more reliable than the guys in girl's manga.'

'But, come on, didn't you notice the smell? It stank so badly I thought I was going to pass out.'

'Yeah they smelled awful, it made me wanna puke.'

'The volleyball club locker room smells the same way.'

'No, it doesn't.'

Everyone was so revved up.

But I was miles away, lost in my own thoughts.

At dawn I sat by the window.

It had become a habit of mine to wait there, whether he ended up coming or not.

Today was the day – I was going to say something. I was determined to make friends with him. Obviously I had decided not to go school. I couldn't let Grandma or Asako find out, though, so I'd asked Maki to deliver the message.

'Why aren'tcha coming?'

'I've decided to become a juvenile delinquent.'

Maki gave a weird chuckle and accepted the mission. I had no doubt she'd be able to pull it off.

The boy appeared around the same time as usual. He mimicked a birdcall below my window, so that my sister wouldn't suspect anything. She was always talking about how she couldn't sleep, though, and she'd finally got some illicit sleeping pills from a pharmacist friend of hers, so it was probably fine anyway. And Grandma is conveniently hard of hearing.

I wrote 'I'm coming down, wait there' on a scrap of paper and dropped it to him. He read the note, put it in his pocket, and gave me a big thumbs-up.

I snuck down the stairs, clutching the big bag I always carry with me. The staircase creaked with every step.

'What's your name?' I asked the waiting boy in a hushed voice.

'Hiro,' he replied simply, and started walking.

'You're a man, aren't you?'

I fell into step beside him. He was much taller than me, which I hadn't been able to tell when I was looking down on him from the second floor.

'Yup.'

'Then, how come you're hanging around here? Males are supposed to be in the Occupancy Zone, aren't they?'

'Shh!' He put a finger to his lips.

He walked quickly, and I had a hard time keeping up.

We didn't have to go far before the houses started to peter out, giving way to fields and the overgrown ruins of old factories. He seemed to want to steer us away from places where we might run into someone.

'Wanna come to my house?' he asked as we walked along the wall of an automobile plant that had shut down long, long ago. I nodded. I really couldn't say why, but I was suddenly overjoyed.

'You can't tell anyone else about it.' In spite of this admonition, it was clear he had trusted me from the start. 'I don't have a home of my own, so I'm borrowing this place.'

He ducked into the automobile plant through a break in the wall. Somewhat removed from the main building was a small shack, like a school custodian's office or a night watchman's room. He headed towards it.

'I almost never go outside. That's why it was such a stroke of luck that I met you. Sometimes I want to go out dressed as a boy so badly I can't help myself, but I only do it maybe once a month, and always in the middle of the night.'

'Once a month?' I repeated. He locked the door from the inside. It was dark. There were windows in two of the walls, but the shutters were closed.

'Yeah. But after you gave me that rabbit, I sort of started to feel like I wanted to see you again right away. So I went out anyway, over and over again. Even though it was risky. I'm lucky I never got caught. Gives me the chills right now just thinking about it.'

There seemed to be two rooms. He took off his shoes, then picked them up. I did the same.

'You don't have to. Since they're girl shoes,' he laughed. 'These shoes, they belonged to my father. They're still a little big on me.'

'Fah-thur?'

'It means a male parent.'

'Wait, a man can be a parent?' I was taken aback and kind of appalled, and my voice came out sounding idiotic. Did that mean that being involved in reproduction was all it took to be a parent?

'Uh-huh. You must have a male parent yourself,' he said calmly.

'No way. I don't even have a mother.'

'But you used to, right?' Hiro was laughing.

I suddenly wanted him to know everything about me, so I started blabbering about my family and school and stuff.

'This "sister" of yours, are you related by blood?'

I was startled by how perceptive Hiro's question was. My mother had been living with my grandma, unmarried, but she'd adopted a child. That was my sister. Me she gave birth to herself.

'Knew it. Can't hide something like that. I mean come on, two women can't make a baby, no matter how long they live together.'

'Obviously. They make them at the hospital.'

'But if a man and a woman are living together, they can make one naturally.'

Which is exactly why the males have to be kept in the GETO. If they were allowed to roam free, the radiation or whatever it is they emit would make all the women around them pregnant.

When I voiced this thought, though, he laughed at me. 'That's the stupidest thing I've ever heard.' Hiro had been laughing pretty much the whole time.

'Why are you laughing?'

'Because being with you is fun.'

'Why do you live in a place like this?'

'Because I ran away from home, obviously.'

'Where's your mother?'

'She lives near here. Not so far from your house, actually. When I go out during the day, I wear girl's clothes, it's safer that way. But I can't stand skirts. When I was little, I didn't mind dressing up like a girl at all, though.'

Hiro said he didn't know where she'd found him, but his mother had been living with a man. Apparently, he stayed hidden up in the attic so no one would find out. It was a big place on the outskirts of town and the neighbours were pretty far away, so he would go for walks in the garden at night. Then one winter he died of some disease. They couldn't take him to the doctor, naturally.

When she got pregnant, his mother had asked a friend who worked at the hospital to forge a permit for her. Then a few years later the other woman had used that favour to blackmail her.

'In your case, they probably couldn't arrange a permit like that. Take a look at the birthplace listed in your family register sometime. I bet it gives the address of the detention centre where your mother's being held.'

I had even opened up to him about that. But because he'd shown himself to me, he was vulnerable too, so I wasn't worried.

When it got to be around noon, Hiro got out some bread and juice. Apparently, his mother brought him food sometimes, and other times he would go out and buy it himself, dressed as a girl.

When we were finished, I took a cigarette out of my bag. He told me he'd never smoked one, and I showed him how. It made him dizzy, I guess, and he fell over backwards. He wasn't getting back up, so eventually I leaned over and peered at his face. Suddenly he hugged me, then flipped me over and pinned me down like we were wrestling. At first, I thought he was just messing around. But he wasn't. Not in the slightest. Hiro wasn't messing around at all.

I spent the rest of that day learning the unexpected, dreadful truth about human life. Learning it with my body.

When I got home that evening a little after seven, my sister was already there.

'You're mighty late.'

Without a word, I started to go upstairs.

'What about dinner?'

'I ate at my friend's house.'

I went up to my room and collapsed onto the bed.

'There's something off about this society. Women and women? What kind of a world is that?'

Hiro had said this as I was leaving to go home. He'd been rough, but he had also been tender in his own way. He said it had to stay our secret, but that was obvious. He also said that what we did was natural. Maybe so, but what a dreadful thing it was!

I plunked my elbows down on the desk and spaced out. Then I smoked one of my precious cigarettes.

Asako came in without warning.

'I've been knocking for a while, why didn't you answer? And where did you get that? Aha, so you're the little sneak thief.'

'What do you want?' I replied finally, frowning.

'Grandma's calling for you.'

I stood up lethargically.

Why the hell would Grandma be calling for me at this hour?

'Can't you just tell her I don't feel well?'

'No, I can't,' declared my sister sternly. How could she be so self-assured? There were things in this life she didn't have a clue about. But it's precisely because they don't know about the dreadful stuff that ignorant people are able to be so confident. But that glittering gaze of hers still somehow made me feel small.

'What's wrong with you? You seem out of it.'

'Nothing, I'm fine.'

She could never imagine what I had done. She didn't have the knowledge or experience. In fact, Asako would most likely live out the rest of her life without ever experiencing that dreadful, spine-tingling thing for herself. And she was lucky. I could never tell anyone the unthinkable truth I had learned that afternoon.

Grandma was sitting in an enormous chair, eating candy. Her skirt was immoderately short. So short that when I opened the door, for a second I thought she wasn't wearing one at all.

'I was going through my wardrobe, and I found some of the clothes I used to wear when I was young. What do you think? Funny, huh?'

Was she going senile or something? I shook my head.

'Oh, come on, it's kind of funny.'

'No, it's not.'

Neither of us spoke for a while. I stood by the wall, staring at my slippered feet.

'I'm sorry to say I'm not all that hard of hearing,' Grandma finally said. 'I heard a strange little bird this morning, and it took my granddaughter away with it.'

She must know everything.

'Asako's different, but you're just like your mother. You'd best let that go, though. That man isn't there anymore, anyway.'

Recalling something Hiro had said to me, I was overcome with tears.

This is what he said: 'Humans are animals, we pair up to mate. And two women can't do that, it's gotta be a man and a woman. You and me, for instance, *the two of us*, living out our lives together. Relying on each other. I think my mother was happy. And my father too, of course.'

'What did Mother do?'

I asked my grandma the one question I was never supposed to ask. I had never put it into words before. I was sure that the answer was somehow connected to what Hiro had said.

'The same thing you did, more or less. And because of that, my daughter was taken from me. That time I accepted it because it was what she wanted, and I even helped her, but not this time. Not with you, not at this age. You're safe now, though. I took care of it. I expect that man is already in the Terminal Occupancy Zone by now. Your sister doesn't know anything about it, though, and she doesn't need to, so keep it to yourself.'

I nodded.

'Alright then, I'll show you something neat. Open up that box on the right-hand side of the wardrobe and look inside. Dammit, can't even listen to records in the open anymore.'

Grandma closed the window and put on a record. It was totally unexpected; I'd had no idea we had such a luxury item as a record player in our house.

We sat there until eight, listening to the Rolling Stones and the Blues Project and the Golden Cups.

'What *is* it, anyway?' I asked, thinking about everything that had happened.

'An adolescent fantasy. But it's over now,' my grandma answered in a condescending tone.

When I returned to my room, I noticed that my anguish was almost entirely gone. Women and women. Just as it should be. But now that I've learned about that thing, I know I'll think of it often. For the next ten years. Twenty even. Poor Hiro, though, locked up in the GETO, rendered apathetic and feeble-minded – he might very well forget. I took out my diary. I didn't care anymore, I would write the truth about what had happened that day.

And yet . . . I put the pen down again before I was done. Now that I know about that *thing*, how can I ever be happy? To doubt this world is a crime. Everyone but everyone believes implicitly in this world, in this reality. I and I alone (well, probably not) know the great secret of this existence, and I'll have to live out the rest of my life keeping it at all costs.

Right now, I have no intention of sacrificing my life for some underground resistance movement. But who knows, it might come to that someday.

Shuddering, I turned back to my diary.

Someday, surely someday . . . something will happen. Still shuddering, I finished the entry.

YOU MAY DREAM

My eyes met hers through the glass. She was sitting against the wall, gaze fixed on the front window for who knows how long, waiting. Even when she saw me, she didn't so much as a wave. She just kept staring, expression rigid.

I walked through the door and put on a kind smile, no real meaning behind it.

'Why the stiff face?' I asked.

I was a little surprised every time I saw her. She was never as grotesque as I remembered. She probably weighed around sixty-five kilos. Her face wasn't anything to write home about, but she wasn't exactly repulsive either. She looked older than her age, but only because she didn't take good care of her skin. I can't really explain it, but she was perfectly ugly to my mind, probably because there was literally nothing about her that rewarded the eye. I was pretty sure I'd never met anyone so mediocre, so utterly forgettable.

'What's going on?'

'Well . . .'

She'd always been on the pale side, but she was looking more ghostly than usual. There was something feverish in her almost-motionless eyes.

'There's something I need to talk to you about,' she said, toying with her straw.

'So you said.'

I ordered a cup of coffee. Across the table, she was studying the back of her own hands. They looked red and swollen. She was taking her sweet time, and the drawn-out silence wasn't doing anything for me.

'Come on. Spit it ou—'

'I don't know if I can . . .'

She was still staring at her hands.

'Fine, forget it.'

Just get to the point already.

'But I . . .'

What the hell was she going to say? I bit my nails. I was pretty sure she wasn't stalling on purpose. She wasn't the type to take pleasure in making you squirm. She's actually a good soul if you ask me. She'd never given me any reason to look down on her – not that that ever stopped me. We probably had no business being friends in the first place. Not because we didn't vibe or anything. On the contrary, we *really* did – so much that I had to wonder if she wasn't the embodiment of my unconscious.

She lifted her face slowly, then stiffly asked, 'We're good friends, aren't we?'

''Course we are.'

I answered without thinking. For me, a conversation's just a series of reactions, reflex responses. I've got a habit of saying whatever the other person wants to hear. I'm a real people-pleaser. I know it's probably not a good thing, but I accept myself – devil-may-care attitude and all.

'We've known each other for nearly ten years.'

She wanted reassurance.

'Sure, ever since we were kids.'

Good or not, I didn't have any other friends. Ever since I was little, I'd had a hard time getting along with others. That's why they sent (well, *send*) me to the Medical Success Centre. It's still hard for me to hold down a job. I do what I can to help Mum at home. Mum's no slouch when it comes to show costumes — designing them, making them. With age, I guess she's kind of lost her edge and orders have dropped off a little, but . . .

My coffee came. She kept a sticky eye on the back of our waitress until she was out of sight, then turned to look out the window for a solid five seconds. I guessed she was working up to say . . . whatever she had to say. I assumed she'd fallen for some guy who didn't even know she existed. I took a swig of my coffee and it burned my throat. I pulled out my handker-chief and held it to my mouth. She took a slow look around the room and pushed the button at the edge of the table. A see-through capsule popped up to cover us. No one could hear us now.

'What do you think of the Population Department?' she finally asked.

'Where'd that come from? What do you want me to say?'

'Well, you know . . .'

'I mean,' I said cautiously, 'nothing's gonna change, right?'

'But haven't you ever thought about . . . our dignity as human beings?'

'Nope, not once,' I said, trying to end this before it could start, but she wasn't having it.

Looking up at me, she said in a low voice, 'It's unforgivable, what they're doing.'

The last thing I wanted was to get dragged into some totally pointless debate, so – irresponsibly – I just told her what she wanted to hear.

'Yeah, I guess you're right.'

'But we have to do something, anything. We should protest, get them to change the law . . .'

'Ya think?'

Okay, now I get it. She got a slip. She's never said anything about cryosleep before. Not a word.

'The way they're doing this, it doesn't make any sense. You know what I'm saying?'

Sure I did. But saying so wasn't going to change anything now.

'Well, it's a lottery, so . . .'

Now she was getting worked up. She shook her head, then reached into her bag and pulled out a ratty but pristinely folded handkerchief. She took a corner and dabbed neatly at the corner of her eye. If it were me, the same action would have been so sloppy and careless. We really couldn't be more different, the two of us.

'But that isn't true, I'm sure of it. Top government officials are definitely getting special treatment!'

38

If you're so sure, then why bother asking me for my opinion?

'It's so unfair . . .' Her voice started to crack with emotion. 'Don't you think it's unfair?'

'I do, I do.'

She wasn't interested in what I had to say. She was just talking *at* me. But that's the way we'd talk: duelling monologues, each of us in a bubble all her own, no hope of ever going anywhere.

'I know one of the ministers got a slip the other day, but that was a total sham. They're just trying to win the public over. Most people have no idea what's going on. Everyone knows that from an international perspective . . .' Another habit of hers: producing long strings of borrowed thoughts she hasn't bothered digesting.

'Gee whiz, looks like I'm about to get a real wake-up call . . .'

Sarcasm undetected.

'No, that's not . . .' she said, her cheeks a little red. Then she kept on going. 'The Population Control Act went into effect a century ago, but it never should've happened . . .' – she couldn't stop herself now – '. . . law of death . . . crime against humanity . . .' Blah blah blah.

All I could do was wait for her to calm down. She talked and talked and was still miles from making her point, whatever that might be. Still, I played the role of concerned friend, listening to her vent for nearly two fucking hours. Whenever she got that way, I couldn't help but feel like I was just some human-shaped receptacle, there to receive her emotional excreta.

Of all people, though, why me? I'm a far cry from the shoulder-to-cry-on type.

'Hey, do your parents know?'

'I couldn't bring myself to tell them . . . But I guess they got their own notice about it. It's true what they say, being a parent can be a real drag.'

'Yeah, I guess.'

I don't know how much more of this I can take.

'They're losing their minds, both of them. Know what I mean?'

'Sure, I get it.'

Hurry up, already. Yeesh.

'Seeing them in person would've been way too much. I couldn't do it. I mean, who could've seen this coming?'

The words coming out of her mouth are so tragic they're actually comical.

'Come on, no one's gonna die or anything,' I said, trying to console her, but it backfired.

'Same difference! No one who's gone under has ever come back, not once.'

''Course not. It's only been thirty years.'

'And the worst part is all those stupid kids who actually *want* to go under! They go along with the crowd, even though they have no idea what's going on.'

'What, and you do?'

'Hey, I'm not saying I have all the answers. But it's kinda obvious if you think about it. The population's out of control, so they're trying to keep it in check. They act like it's just a little nap or something. It scares me how everyone's so cool about it, but I guess that's the world we live in. Everyone's so numb they can't even take life seriously anymore —'

'Sure, sure.'

'Come on, I'm being serious.'

Did I hurt her feelings?

'Okay, what do you want me to say? Tell me and I'll say it.'

'Now you're making fun of me.'

Wait, she just figured that out *now*?

'Hey, we're not getting anywhere like this.'

'Okay, fine,' she said, putting her hand on her forehead.

I was pretty worn out, but I had to try to get her back on track. 'You had something you wanted to ask me, right?'

'Right. I was wondering if you'd be okay with me transferring . . . to your dreams . . .' She was staring right at me, her question hanging in the air between us.

'Okay. Why not.'

'Huh!'

'"Huh"? You mean you wanted me to say no?'

'No no, you just . . . blurted it out.'

'Want me to reconsider?'

'That's not what I'm saying . . .'

I got it. She wanted me to look deep into her eyes (holding her hands in mine) and give my solemn assent. She was convinced that everything that matters is revealed in big melodramatic moments. She was disappointed to be deprived of her precious climax.

'It's just most people transfer to a family member or a lover. Not that I'm opposed . . .'

'I understand.'

Understand what?

'You know we're total opposites, right? You're okay with that?'

'That's kind of the point. I asked my parents, of course. Neither one of them is much of a dreamer.'

'Everybody dreams. If I dig deep, I can remember at least four dreams a night. The question's whether or not you remember.'

'I guess you're right. That makes sense.'

'You just don't want to be forgotten, do you?'

'Of course I don't! That's the whole idea, right? What's the point of being transferred if you won't even be remembered?'

She was always so quick to agree with everything I said. What a way to live. Were her own thoughts so nebulous they couldn't resist the pull of other people's opinions and ideas?

'I dream every night. It really takes it out of me, too. My dreams are always so fucking vivid.'

'That's why I'm asking you. I mean, we're definitely on the same wavelength.'

'Yeah, I guess so.'

'From the time you get the slip, they give you fifty days. So before they put me under, we'll have to go to the Population Department together. I guess they have these helmets or whatever that they have to put on us.'

'Yeah, I know.'

'It's supposed to take ten minutes or so, wait time included.'

'I bet they're really backed up, what with all the people out there dying to be frozen.'

'Whole families, even. If you're terminally ill, I can get that. But some of them have the craziest reasons. They want their son to be a spaceman or something. Stuff like that.'

'I dunno, kinda makes sense.'

'But not for us. It's way too optimistic. The Population Network is constantly broadcasting images of some perfect metropolis in a future full of nature and all-round prosperity. Most people are so naive they buy it, too. So many kids out there want to be crew members that it's getting seriously competitive. They want to wait until they can make enough ships. They can call it cryosleep all they want, but it's death — they're putting these people to death.'

'So when's good?'

Called back to reality, she balled her handkerchief in her hands.

'Um . . . How about next week? I'll set it up so we can go drinking after.'

Hardly necessary. All we had to do was stop by the nearest office – walk-ins welcome. We could find a bar wherever we went, no problem.

I was feeling worn out again. I should have said no. We're just so different.

Like most people these days, I don't overthink things. I'll go along with whatever. No firm beliefs, no hang-ups. Just a lack of self-confidence tangled up in fatalistic resignation. Whatever the situation, nothing ever reaches me on an emotional level. Nothing's important. Because I won't let it be. I operate on mood alone. No regrets, no looking back.

Before me, the world stretches out flat, smooth and featureless. Gentle and inconstant.

But this friend of mine was a serious stickler. Every single thing she did was awkward, wholly devoid of charm.

We'd been friends for years, but not once had she ever surprised me. I don't care who it is, everyone's got to have a side to them that takes you by surprise, typically something childish: an unexpected purity, naiveté, coldness . . .

Then there was her. No ups, no downs. Living in her own tiny world, clinging to the past, indecisive, maudlin, overemotional.

But it was fine.

It was too much of a hassle to back out now. Why bother? Though I suspected thinking like this was a bad habit of mine, I also reasoned that even if I granted this obstinate soul entry into my mental universe, it'd only be while I was asleep.

'You have time now?' I asked, injecting my voice with a shot of levity, hoping it'd clear the air of bad vibes.

'Sure. You wanna get something to drink?'

'Let's drop by the Population Department first.'

'You mean now? Are you sure?'

'It's not like we have to do anything to get ready. As long as we're sober, whatever works, right?'

'Well, I guess. It's just so sudden . . .'

What was going on in her brain? Why make such a big deal out of some stupid little transfer? It's not like it's a birthday or something.

'It doesn't matter when we do it, right?'

'I know, but . . .'

'Look, if we're gonna do it, why drag our feet? Let's get it over with.'

I pulled out enough money to cover my own coffee, all the while wondering if she'd take it as an insult.

'Don't worry. I've got it,' she said, waving her hand, but I ignored her and stood up.

'Oh, by the way,' I said, 'what happened to that guy from last year? He'd let you transfer, wouldn't he?'

She gulped.

'Forget about him,' she said, her voice high and borderline threatening. 'Just let it go, okay?'

I didn't say anything else. I sighed and followed her out.

I'm standing under a bright blue sky.

In front of me is a path stretching out like a white ribbon, zigzagging over a gentle hill, then disappearing beyond the curve.

It's spring. Just the thought of spring fills me with joy. And it's that much better because there's nobody else around. Slowly, I start walking.

It's so warm here. Feels good. My mind's a total blank. I leave countless shells – sloughed-off selves – in my wake.

In moments like this, I swear I can almost feel eternity.

Someone's behind me.

Didn't see that coming.

Eyes. I can feel a sticky gaze on my back. When something creeps up behind you like that, it can only be the past – or an enemy. Darkness, something incomprehensible.

And on a beautiful day like this . . . I almost click my tongue. The air behind me is heavy. I feel something warm on my neck, something like an animal's breath.

Pulled by an invisible string, I spin around.

It's her.

She's just standing there, looking clueless.

Why'd she appear right behind me like that? Why not up ahead or off to the side?

—You scared me! It's been two months.

—They put me under yesterday. That's why I'm here now, or at least my consciousness is.

Huh. So this is a dream.

—How do you feel?

—Pretty good, actually. Loads lighter.

—Funny, you look just as heavy to me.

—Because that's how you see me.

—Think so?

—It's not just me. This whole world is yours. You're responsible for all you see.

What the hell? She appears out of nowhere and starts telling me how everything's my responsibility?

—Hey, if you don't like it, no one's forcing you to stick around.

—That's not what I said.

—Do what you want. This is the world for me, though.

Just feel it, the soft light of the sun. It's like an invisible scarf.

—Sorry, I didn't mean it. I like what you've done with the weather. And it's really good to see you.

Guess she's in a good mood.

—Likewise.

Not really, but I can play along all the same.

—But this place is way too dry.

—Oh yeah? I don't really have anything to compare it against.

—Mine's wetter, a gentler world.

—Well, well, well . . .

46

—And it's bright here, too bright.

Why'd she bother saying sorry if she was just going to keep on nagging? What's her deal?

That instant, the sky changes colour like nothing I've ever seen.

—Wh-what was that?

—It changed, just the way you wanted it.

But that isn't true. The sky is mirroring my mood.

—Whoa! Things can change that quickly? Kinda scary.

Well – I start to say – don't get all mushy on me now, but I bite my tongue. If this is where we're starting, it's pretty easy to see where we're heading.

Low and ominous, dark clouds rush by at frightening speed, roaring like a dragon clearing its throat. How would she react if Wagner started playing and a black fortress appeared out of nowhere?

My mood has soured in no time. No surprises there. I guess I usually end up like this when I'm with her.

The sky settles into a smudgy charcoal, the diffuse light of the sun blurring the edges of the landscape all around us.

Lacking the will to walk further, I sit down on the grass. She plants herself beside me and starts futzing with her skirt.

—Hey, what's that?

—A robot from when I was a kid. He was at the Centre, but that was maybe twenty years ago. Wonder what he's doing here.

The robot wheezes closer, wheels spinning, lights on his head blinking. He's the most primitive model — the kind kids go nuts for. He makes a noise like a fuzz guitar, like he's saying LET'S PLAY TOGETHER.

47

—I spent a whole lot of time with this robot. He was my only friend.

She's making me dig up childhood memories. I'm a hard-core people-pleaser, even in my dreams.

—Wow!

Is she actually blushing? She's such a sucker for schmaltz. It's like she gets drunk on emotion, like it's a religion for her.

—That's love for you. It's always there, deep inside our hearts.

That kind of sentimental bullshit always kills my buzz.

I reach out and flick the robot. It's reduced to a pile of rubbish in an instant. Nothing inside.

The look of shock on her face. Then that shock turns to sadness. I can see it in her eyes. Whatever. Like I even care.

—It must have been hard for you, going so long without love.

—Listen to the words coming out of your mouth! If I ever said something so sappy, I'd bite off my tongue and die of embarrassment. There are laws against saying stuff like that in this world.

I'm just making it up as I go.

—Wait, what?

—Seriously. The Ban on Sentimentality. Break it and you'll dissolve into nothingness. Your perspective will linger on a little, then even that'll dry up and get blown away by the wind. Like that! Poof, and you're gone.

—Hold on, that's insane. I mean, I just got here. Now you're saying it's my way or the highway? Nobody can change just like that.

She's trying to smile, but it looks more like she's having a stroke. I want to say something, to make some snide remark, but can't bring myself to do it. Same as always. She doesn't get jokes anyway, so what's the point?

I'm repulsed by my own nastiness. Nothing like that's ever happened before.

I've always enjoyed making fun of other people, cornering them. But now that she's here, the whole world feels different. I've always been so soft, but I can feel myself hardening up.

Does she stand for so-called goodness and morality in this place? I guess she's always had that side to her, even in the waking world. She was always saying, 'Don't do that . . . It has to be this way . . . That's unforgivable.'

But her power's not without limits. When I put my foot down, she abides. Later on, she'll start griping ad nauseam, but I can usually tune her out.

Maybe she corresponds to my underdeveloped unconscious. Maybe she's like my shadow. Which I guess means I'm her shadow. Together, the two of us form a whole.

What one lacks, the other brings to the table.

A groan wells up in my throat. I lie back on the grass, utterly deflated. God, how simplistic.

She came right up next to me, like a bride approaching the altar.

Now I understood why our relationship turned out the way it did, her looking after my every little need. On trips together, as soon as we'd reach the hotel room, she'd make tea, wipe down the table, hang up my dresses. What a pain, I'd tell myself, all the while letting her do it anyway.

—What are you going to do now? What's going to happen?

Who knows, I reply, not giving it any real thought.

—That's kinda scary.

—Being scared isn't gonna change anything.

What else could I say?

—Hey, it's getting darker, isn't it?

—Sure is.

How long can she keep going on like this?

—Is the sun going down?

—Nope.

—Then what's going on?

—REM sleep's ending.

—What happens then? What happens to me?

—You disappear.

—But I don't want to disappear.

—It doesn't matter what you want. You'll vanish as soon as I wake up.

—Okay. See you again, right?

What – I mutter under my breath – from now on? Forever?

Un-cha-cha un-cha. A repulsive melody blared inside me. An awful ostinato. I woke up.

The vision slowly loosened its fearsome grip. It lost its colour, like a faded photograph, and then vanished in the dark.

I took a deep breath.

In the waking world, I obsess over the superficial. I devote myself to the acme of emptiness. And that devotion infiltrates my dreams, the world of my unconscious. Covered in thick plastic – that's how I've made myself. Over years and years. The sadistic act of self-creation.

The sudden arrival of this shadow threatened the balance. She infused a syrupy wetness into my world. I'm better off on my own, I tell myself again and again. What's she trying to do? I guess it wasn't that hard to figure out. Within the realm of the mind, the emotions that guide her behaviour are just as rational as reasoned thought. That being the case, I could calculate the results of any emotion she might have. If she tried to keep the feeling down, she'd just flip a pig. First law of thermodynamics.

The only reason she can do what she does is because she doesn't know the first thing about self-control. Yeesh. There's no way I can do this every morning. No way. The dream was slow to fade – I could still feel the breath of the beast on me. It had always been such a merciless world before, too. So bright, so dry.

I guess it was good I went to sleep last night with my body-phone on. I was about to take the pendant off when the world's most shameless guitar rang out. The heinous sound made me shudder. My leg shot up, sending my blanket up into the air.

I laughed. What I wouldn't give to take a look inside the head of the person who programmed this stuff. That'd make life more fun.

I headed into the kitchen with my bodyphone playing and made coffee. Surrendering myself to the ridiculous rhythm, I pulled out a paper filter. Nothing beats the old way. That's what tastes best.

With the hot mug in my hands, I went into Mum's room. She was already awake, just staring at the ceiling.

'There's that face again!'

I handed her the mug of coffee, grinning like a fool.

'Hey, what did you expect? At my age, when I wake up, I need a minute to sit here and just sigh at . . . I don't know, the heartless logic of this world.'

'You mean time?'

'Yeah, time. It's all I have, and it's a big fat void. Sounds sad, right? But it's not. And that's what makes me so sad. Know what I mean?'

'Sure I do. I'm pretty much over the hill myself.'

'Come on, don't start with that again.'

'Start with what? It's all downhill after twenty-five! And, you know, looking back is fine and all, but it's awful when you turn to look forward only to see yourself looking back.'

'You're not making any sense, honey. Hey, a call came earlier. I was barely awake, so I left the cam off, but there was this tiny man on the other end. It wasn't how I wanted to start the morning, eye to eye with this shorty.'

'Takes one to know one. What'd the guy say?'

'He asked if that friend of yours went into cryosleep. I told him I wasn't sure.'

'Oh, that guy. That's her boyfriend. A real catch, right? Well, I guess they deserve each other. He's such a freak. I dunno, maybe he's not that bad. If that's her thing, though, she'd be better off going out with a dog.'

'You're joking, right? You're such a phony,' Mum said, a smirk on her face.

I sat on the floor.

'Yeah, obviously. I'm cursed, incapable of being serious with anybody. I could never say something like that and mean it. Just said it for kicks. No other intentions, base or otherwise.'

'Maybe he'll call again later.'

Mum threw on her gown and started looking around for her slippers.

'He's got to be wondering about her.'

'Hey, keeping somebody under costs money, right? I wonder if the Population Department can stay in the black.'

'They're saying they can. What with their new methods and everything.'

'That's what they say, sure.'

'Exactly. But maybe all those people are actually dead. The doctors at the Population Department show us all this data and swear that's not the case, but who knows? We won't know anything for sure until they're unfrozen, and that's waaay in the future.'

'Hey, you okay? You look zapped.'

I picked at the carpet, saying nothing.

I killed that robot at the Centre ages ago. She made me remember that. The fact that I have zero remorse makes me feel weirdly cold — and sad. Dreaming every night was draining me. I could see her accusing finger pointed right at me. I horrified her. She's probably itching to throw herself into some classical tragedy.

'Do you really have to work today?' I asked, mustering all the sweetness I could.

'As if I have a choice . . .'

'Aw, come on. Work's the worst. What if we took a day off? We can live like a couple of bedridden biddies and have a good old-fashioned nap-off.'

'You're getting a whole lot of sleep these days.'

'But I always wake up tired, no matter how much sleep I get. I'm so worn-out that I go back to bed early. Then I dream, and my dreams wear me out again.'

'Honey, it sounds like you hate this friend of yours.'

'Not at all.'

Mum set her mug down on the bedside table and lost herself in thought.

'Did you talk to the doctor at the Centre?'

'I told him everything. But lately it all feels so moronic. I mean, why should I bare my soul to this guy? Think about it. We don't even know each other.'

I did like him once. He was basically a stand-in for my father, but he turned out to be completely useless. He never did anything for me. Still, I guess he filled a certain role for a little while. But I no longer had a need for him. Where the hell was I heading now? I was always moving from one attachment object to the next, no end in sight.

And Yoshiko probably thought that made me dangerous. It scared her.

'You feeling okay, honey?'

She's worried. Poor momma. How'd she wind up with a daughter like me?

'Your head's full of sawdust, like the stuff those dolls are made of,' Mum said. 'You're like a composition doll.'

I felt even worse now than when I got up. Music wasn't working. I turned off my pendant, killing the sound no one else could hear.

'Isn't there some way to keep yourself from dreaming?'

'There is. But you'll go insane if you keep it up. Schizophrenics are fine without REM sleep because they dream during the day, with their eyes open.'

Mum frowned at me.

'Hey, wanna eat?' A necessary change of subject.

'What's going on with you these days? All you ever want to do is eat. You sick?'

Mum went into the kitchen.

'Sick of not having a man in my life.' I tried making Mum laugh, but I missed the mark. Staggering to my feet, I dragged myself to the dining table.

'I thought you had a guy.'

'I got bored.'

'Did something happen?'

'Don't be stupid, Mum. Nothing happened – that's why I was bored. He didn't do anything wrong. Nothing. I'm just beyond it. I guess I've achieved enlightenment.'

'Yeah, right.' This time she laughed. I could tell by the way her back shook.

Ever since Yoshiko started showing up in my dreams, all I wanted was more sleep, more food. Did I want to die? No, that wasn't it.

The phone rang.

I went to the screen and flicked the switch. Even that took it out of me. The doctor's face appeared in front of me.

'Oh, good morning.'

He bobbed his head a little like he was sorry to bother me. I did the same in return.

'It's been a while since we've seen you at the Centre. Is

everything okay? Do you want to put our meetings on hold for a little while?'

'It's just' – suddenly I was a child again – 'there's no point.'

'Geez! Will you listen to this kid,' Mum muttered, twisting her neck to look at me.

'Why would you say that?' The doctor blinked.

'Because I don't need a cure, even if I am sick.'

'But you're not sick.'

'What difference does it make? I'm so wiped. All I mean is, I think I've made my peace. Like, I'm fine the way I am.'

Safe to say I'm definitely not.

'If that's how you feel . . .'

The doctor looked down for a second, then lifted his head again.

'Well, you should come visit whenever you're feeling up to it. Are you working?'

'Not really, no.'

'Then how about next Friday morning? If you're heading somewhere else, maybe you could stop by.'

Why's he being so polite? Poor guy. What the hell's going on with me? Why am I taking pity on everybody this morning?

'I'll see what I can do,' I said softly, ashamed.

'Well, I'll be waiting. Take care.'

Then the screen went dark. Like a fading dream.

Mum started setting out cups and plates.

'You've been like this ever since the transfer, a shadow of your former self.'

Mum took some time to think, then continued, 'What if you had them erase her? Could you?'

'Yeah, any time.'

'Well, maybe you should.'

'Not yet. I still wanna see where this goes. I kinda feel like something's gonna happen, something crazy.'

'You always want to see how far you can push things — it's gonna be your downfall.'

'Yeah, you may be right,' I said as I started stuffing myself.

'From the sound of it, she's not a bad person.'

'That's what makes it so hard. The whole thing really bums me out, but I guess it kinda appeals to me, too, almost like a game. It's like, who has more willpower, you know? Except it's my dream, so it's a little unfair. Still, nothing goes the way I want, either, so maybe things are actually more balanced than I thought.'

'Just forget about work. What if you went roller skating?'

'Yeah, that's what Lucky said.'

'That guy keeps on calling, huh?'

'He's cute, like a puppy. Simple and cheerful and full of energy. A while back, we were going through the park at night and it was a full moon, so Lucky got down on all fours, looked up at the moon and started howling. God, I looove that side of him.'

I cracked a smile. I honestly felt that way, but there wasn't any spark there. It was more like I was looking down on him from a great height.

'So why don't you call him? He's got nothing else going for him, other than being a good kid, but he's way better than the other boys. Taller, too.'

I almost gagged on my soup. Height is all she cares about when it comes to boys. Height first, then smarts. For me, I don't care that much about brains. What really matters is how much the guy listens to me. Of course, I don't act that way with Lucky. It's never even crossed my mind to try to get him to understand me. All I ever think about is how I can trick him. I know, 'trick him' is a funny way to put it. I just want us to have fun together while we can. But I can feel my desire to be with him slipping.

When we were done eating and I was getting changed, the phone rang. It was Lucky.

'How's it going?'

He always seems so happy.

'Like this,' I said, switching on my cam. I unbuttoned my blouse so he could see the lacy bra he'd given me. Why was this guy sending me this kind of stuff anyway?

'Whoa, whoa. Put 'em away! I'm with Buddy Boy.'

I buttoned up.

'Why aren't you guys at school?'

'We bailed. You get my tapes?'

'Yeah. They were insanely good. My favourite's the one with all the vile, ear-splitting tracks.'

'I bet they had you flapping around like a fish out of water.'

'Oh, I thought I was gonna die!'

Please, please stay this way forever, I thought. Always happy — never sad, never serious, never in pain. It'd mean the world to me, just to know you can go on being the way you are. Far, far away from me.

'And that's what they call art. I have no idea what they're trying to say, making music like that. Makes you wonder what they were thinking, huh?'

Lucky would just glide right on, same as always. He would get into all kinds of things but never go deep. All his value was right there on the surface. And that was why Mum thought he was such a playboy.

'I can't go out today.' I almost wanted to tell him why, but it was too much trouble.

'Why not?'

'You wouldn't understand. It's an adult thing.'

'Pssh, I'm only two years younger than you.'

'You're young for your age, Lucky. And that's what I like about you.'

I meant it, too. This was no act. But I could feel a comfortable distance growing between us. Which was fine.

'Hey, we're gonna be at this guy's house later.' He grabbed Buddy from off cam. 'You know the place, right? Don't keep us waiting. Cool?'

He always had the weirdest way of talking – brutal one second, sweet the next. Before I knew it, I was nodding.

Where am I? Standing in a dim corridor, inside what seems to be some gigantic building. I'm barefoot, in a bathrobe.

There are doors all around me, but they don't touch the floor, don't reach the ceiling. Every one of them is the entrance to a shower stall.

I start walking, my bare feet slapping against the floor. I don't know where I'm heading, but I guess I'm looking for a way out. I start at the far end, opening the doors one at a time. Nobody anywhere. When I turn a corner, all I see is more doors. Another hallway, cold and wet.

It reminds me of her. She's got to be close.

I nudge open another door half-heartedly, then pull it shut before moving on to the next. So weird how they're all shower stalls.

Then she came out of the darkness in the same overalls as always. Every time I see her, she's wearing the exact same thing. I'm sure she had a few different looks in the waking world, but I guess I couldn't tell them apart. She really loves her greys and browns, the duller the better.

— I've been looking for you.

She's winded. What's she all worked up for?

— Having a hard time on your own?

Not like I was blaming her or anything.

— I'm an introvert and introverts need companions.

Right. I forgot about that habit she had (yes, *had*) of stringing words together like they were actually comprehensible. More than that, there was something sharp lurking in what she said.

Look at her make-up. A throwback to another era. Blue eyelids and red lips leaping off her otherwise drab face. What a train wreck.

I think it was an ex of hers who said it: She's got no style when it comes to clothes or make-up. And I'm pretty sure I shot back, 'So what kind of style's she got?'

Oh, right. I have something to tell her.

— Your man called this morning.

The second I deliver the message, she brightens up.

— What did he say?

Whoa, chill out. Nothing to get excited about.

— My mum picked up, so . . .

I feel sorry for her.

—He didn't call back later?

—Nope.

I didn't want to tell her that. I feel like there's a snake inside me. I hate it. It wasn't like this before the transfer. I used to be so empty inside, so pure.

—What are you trying to say?

Don't ask me when you already know the answer. No, wait – it's a scary thought, but maybe I'm the only one who knows.

—He probably wanted some . . . reassurance.

—What's that supposed to mean?

I can see the defiance in her eyes. No, not defiance — hatred. She hates me. That's why she keeps showing up like this. *What's that supposed to mean?* God, the mileage she's had out of that line.

—You know, he wanted to make sure you went under.

—What the fuck are you trying to say?

She squares her shoulders. Why can't she just let it go? I only said what I said to put a little fear in her (if that's even why I did it), but at this point she's got zero pride left. And she's the one always saying there's nothing more important than pride.

—You really want me to say more? He's scared you're gonna come back, that you're gonna stab him or something.

—Why would I do that?

Her voice is actually trembling.

—I get why he's scared. I mean, when things started getting crazy, you were crying every time I saw you. I know it was pretty serious and all, but you only saw him once a week — five, six times total? But that didn't stop you from unburdening your soul and confessing your undying love for him (which she actually did — he told me so). You really put your obsession out there for all to see.

Before him, nothing dramatic ever happened to her. So she had to dream things up. And now it's become a complex of hers (apparently) — that nothing ever happened.

—I don't wanna hear it.

There was a petulant bloodlust in her voice.

We just stood there, speechless.

A low rumble was coming from somewhere — an air conditioner or maybe a boiler.

Guess there isn't anyone else around.

She always loved gossip. Celebrity stuff. Something's up with those two, she'd say, unable to contain her giddy excitement. The way she idolized the girls was downright weird. Falling for the boys would have been a lot more normal, but she'd go on and on about the girls for hours — almost like she'd taken their place.

Life's never satisfied her. No, that's not exactly right. She half resents her past but can't bring herself to let it go. She relives her regret, over and over. Nothing happened, I did nothing.

She leaves her physical self behind, entering some resplendent other. I guess it never occurred to her that she might be able to function in reality if she could just get over her self-effacing transference.

She's always wanted to forget her own wretchedness, even if only for a second. She couldn't have made it this far without constantly identifying with other people.

—Knock it off already. I swear, it's like you were born an old maid.

The words just came out. I have even less self-control here than in the waking world.

She shot me a look. It was hardly homicidal, but the strength of her spite was obvious enough.

—Don't you get it? You've had a huge influence on me.

—I had no idea, but I guess I can see it now.

I wish I hadn't, but I said it, just like that.

—I used to be . . . obsessed. Seriously.

There was something sticky in her voice.

—News to me!

I really shouldn't be so glib.

—And that's why, we need to settle this.

—Settle what?

—My feelings. You've got to make this right.

My, my. What a scary thing to say. I can feel it again. Something hanging in the air.

—What do you think's going on outside this building?

—How would I know? It's your world.

—I bet we're in a bomb shelter and most of the human race has died off.

She shuddered.

—Hey, what are you doing? I have the right to choose our environment, too.

I didn't say anything. I just started walking and she followed. The corridors were a maze. First things first, we had to get away from the centre. It would be great if we had some string or maybe a piece of chalk.

I had no way of knowing if we were getting any closer to an exit, but I kept on walking. All I found were identical doors, floating amid the same unchanging light.

—Looks like your mind's a real mess.

Is she taking the piss?

—Yeah, who knew I was such a labyrinth.

The walls changed colour. I got the feeling they were fragile, like they were made of packed earth. Maybe we were getting closer to the exit. Maybe this maze had been abandoned for centuries.

—Hey, I bet we can break through this.

I started kicking at the wall, but I was barefoot, so it didn't do any good.

—Stop! What are you doing?

—What do you think I'm doing? Trying to get out. I thought you hated this place.

—But it's dangerous.

—Yeesh, you're afraid of everything, aren't you?

When I threw myself into the wall, it came crumbling down. She shrieked.

On the other side of the wall we found an empty room made of mud. One window. Outside, I could see the blue of dawn. We'd made it to the outer wall.

In one corner, there was a huddle of people so dirty I couldn't even tell if they were men or women. They were in rags, skinny and covered in grime. They had faces like rats and ate like rats. I guess they weren't human after all.

She kept poking me in the side. I think she was trying to tell me to stay away, but I walked right over to talk to them.

Their responses were obscure, but not indecipherable. I asked them question after question about the outside world, until eventually I learned that they'd lived through some kind of apocalypse. Far from here, there are human survivors, the rat people said to me. We know because we're telepathic.

—We'd better go and check it out.

—Wait, we don't even know what happened. What if there's radiation out there? Or ammonia storms? We don't even know for sure if we're on Earth.

I guess she's right about that.

—Look, the window. There's a crack in it, so the air's got to be fine.

I walked away from the room. It looked like the building was buried under a gentle hill. The corridors weren't corridors anymore. More like a cave system.

Timidly, I made my way toward the source of the cold, white light. I could see a storm outside the cave. The sea was close. Trees that looked like black palms were blowing in the wind. There was a narrow trail of clay so weather-beaten it was almost gone in places. I could tell we were at the edge of an inlet.

—There are people, way over there. That's where I want to go, but there's no way in hell . . .

The more I talk with her, the more I sound like a boy. Even though it's not like that when we argue. She starts clinging to me.

—Is this the end of the world?

Calm down. It's not like you're the only one who's scared here.

—I dunno.

—What were you thinking? Why'd you destroy the world?

—It's not like all life has been wiped out!

—*Those* aren't human beings. Hey, do you think it was a nuclear war?

—No way. I have a feeling this world is in another dimension.

—So what do you think happened?

I don't know how to respond. I'm afraid that if I voiced the doubts spreading inside me like ink, they might become real.

The kind of light you see before the dawn, its brightness unchanging . . .

We were standing at the top of a hill. All around us was a waste-land of red earth. This planet has to be extremely small — there's a roundness to the horizon.

She couldn't speak for a while. It was all too much.

The sky hanging over our heads had transformed into a dome. Harsh, mineral light covered every inch of the hard blue surface. At the centre of it all was a pasted yellow sun that looked like cheese. It had a cruelty to it, like a giant eye glaring down at the beings on the surface.

—This place is terrible.

She spoke at last.

Each ray of light was like a needle, offering no warmth, but it was so bright it stung. Nothing in this place had a shadow.

—I wish there were people here.

—Even if there were, they probably wouldn't be any help.

—Still, I wish there were people.

Maybe she got her wish. Slowly, I turned around and saw a group of humans – maybe fifty or sixty of them, crawling along the earth like ants. What was this? Forced labour?

I heard a siren blaring somewhere, announcing some catastrophe.

—All this nothingness . . . It's horrible.

—One time, I was in a town with light like this, but it was a town. Still, I could tell all the buildings were just some kind of backdrop. When I looked at the backs, they were nothing but plywood. The sky was an ominous purple. The roads were packed with people and cars, though.

—Don't tell me you like this kind of world.

—I don't hate it.

—Why not? It doesn't make any sense!

—Beats me. I can't explain it.

—What's there to like about a place like this?

—For starters, look at how immaculate it is. This light blanches everything.

—You're out to annihilate the human race!

—Yeesh, you sound like a broken record. The thought's never even crossed my mind!

—Is there no real life left in your world? No friends? No school? Do you hate those things?

—You kidding? I love them.

While I fielded her questions, I had to ask myself: What was it about her that was turning me into a man? Got to be all that femininity. She's acting like such a woman (as society defines the role, anyway) that I have to play the man just to keep the balance. What if I ran into a boy? Could I even play the part of a woman?

I don't need any men here — not Lucky, not the doctor, nobody. I've already got everything I need.

Syzygy? Androgyny? I'm no man and I'm no woman. Who needs gender anyway? I just want to get out of this place, to be on my own.

I've got no desire to see the collapse of humankind or the end of the world. I just want everyone to enjoy their lives. That's why I came here — to a different time stream, a different planet, a different universe.

—You hate this world, don't you?

I asked with sympathy.

—Yeah, I hate it.

She's still pissed off. Poor thing. She really has zero grasp on the situation.

Here, in this place, you're only a shadow.

—I don't know how it got this way. It wasn't like this before, not until you came along.

—You mean it's my fault?

—That's not what I'm saying. But why can't you just stop caring?

—Like you don't care? That's bull. You've got your own likes and dislikes, too. Even when it comes to people.

—'Course I do. It's all light and shadow, practically nothing in the middle. And I get a kick out of making fun of the people I hate. But, on a more basic level, I don't care. I don't care and that's what makes it so fun.

—All at the same time?

—Yeah, all at the same time.

—And it's always been like that?

—Ever since I was little. Don't get me wrong, I have all these emotions inside. I get angry all the time. But if I try to think about why I feel that way, there's no real reason. I just get angry cause I'm bored.

—Does that go for everything you do? It's so unnatural.

—I guess it does, so it's natural for me. Everything feels serious, and everything feels like a pose, not that it really makes any difference. I can act all kinds of ways, but in the end it's always an act.

—What about the real you? Aren't you just repressing your true nature?

—That's what I'm saying. This is the real me, this is who I am.

—That's the saddest thing I ever heard. To think that's the only way you can live.

—It doesn't make any difference, though. I mean, who cares?

The needling light was unchanging. What if this planet's sun is just a ridiculously powerful light bulb? That'd explain why it isn't moving. But if it doesn't move . . . What about time? Had it stopped?

—You're off your rocker.

—Yeah, rockin' and rollin'. Doesn't bother me.

There was a line running straight across the blue firmament, like someone was slicing the dome in two from the outside with a giant razor.

A thin black line rose slowly from the horizon.

—What is this? What are you doing?

—Don't ask me.

She always wanted to attach motives to everything. Otherwise she couldn't relax.

The invisible razor cut right through the flat clump of yellow sun.

—I can't live in a world like this!

Her whole body was trembling. I'd seen her like this once before, in the waking world. I went to her house one day, and we were just sitting at the dining table, talking, when she started convulsing like crazy. This wasn't your average twitch. It was some real fork-in-socket stuff. I wanted to say something, but I got the feeling she didn't even know what she was doing, so I decided against it.

There was one other reason I kept quiet, too. I was afraid. She really had no idea what was going on – she just kept talking about her favourite celebrity, shaking the whole time. That really scared the hell out of me.

I remember thinking how if she ever went crazy, she'd be the type to sink into some murky abyss without even realizing it. Even our madnesses were opposite. For me, it was always a conscious thing. I wanted to be this way — and that's why I dispatched myself to this far-flung world.

—Hey, you can do whatever you want.

I couldn't take all the talk. I looked up at the sky. At the beautiful hard dome, split clean in two. And when it opens up, on the other side . . . a black, empty, sinister void . . . if I can just make it there, maybe time will . . .

A slip came for me.

Choose? I don't want to choose anything.

When I put the piece of paper on the table and cradled my head, Mum came over.

'Wanna make a run for it? Momma will figure something out.'

A long time ago (when was that?) I felt pity for this person. If I were the same person I was then, I would have felt the same, I'm sure of it. But I'm different now, never feeling anything.

'Hey. Talk to me.'

The woman who gave birth to me peeled my fingers off my head. Softly, too – one at a time.

'My head hurts,' I said in a hoarse whisper.

'I know. You don't want to go under.'

'It's not that,' I said, shaking my aching head slightly.

'What is it?'

'A purely physiological pain.'

She never came back to my dream world again. There was no merging of shadows inside me, either. I had her erased. Now she lives in somebody else's dreams. I was alone again, in my own twisted world, unbothered by all other forms of life. I felt whole again.

Same as in this world, I could feel my own heart stop. That had been going on for some time, even during the day. There were times when I lost all feeling, when I truly felt nothing. I felt like I could do anything — even kill someone. It happened once a year or so. Then when my emotions would start up again, I'd shudder at my own heartlessness . . . But that would fade over time . . . In my dreams, there was nothing holding me back, and that was where I truly felt free.

My head hurt because every time I go to sleep I stare right into that blinding light, never even blinking.

'It's okay, though. I'm feeling a little better.'

I took my hands off my head and looked at Mum. What a cute face she's got.

'I wish it came to me instead.'

She's talking about the slip. But of course it came to me, of course it did.

'Hey,' I said, remembering I had something to say.

'What?'

'Don't hate me, but I'm not going to transfer into your dreams.'

'So who are you . . .?'

'No, I don't want to be in anybody's dreams. I want to go someplace where there's nothing.'

My mental work was over now. All thanks to Yoshiko.

'You . . .'

'Come on, don't say anything embarrassing. Nothing about self-destruction or despair, okay? It's not like that, not at all.'

I just want them all to stay sunny — Mum, Lucky, the doctor. It doesn't bother me that I'm not going to see them anymore, not even a little. Different kinds of people belong in different kinds of worlds. And, lucky enough for me, mine's a world within reach.

I want to keep on living. Forever. And that's how it's going to be. I'll become a lone eye somewhere, floating, without consciousness.

'Your soul's not like mine, is it? It's really something else,' Mum said.

'Yeah,' I said, softly. 'Something nowhere near as good.'

NIGHT PICNIC

Junior's dad came in while he was studying at his desk.

'Well? How's it coming along?'

Dad looked over Junior's shoulder, mouthing a cigarette.

'Good . . . Hey, aren't you supposed to light those things?'

'Oh, right. I keep forgetting.'

Dad produced a lighter from his pocket and lit the cigarette. He drew the smoke into his lungs.

'Come on, Dad. You're the one who's always saying that we can't forget to act like Earthlings.'

'Got me there. Sorry, son . . . I know it's up to me to set a good example for the family. As Earthlings, it's our responsibility, regardless of the time or place, to carry on our way of life. To be the very model of a family. Especially since we're so far away from Earth, out here on our own.'

'Yeah. I guess you're right.'

He examined his father's outfit.

Dad wore a black double-breasted suit, paired with a black

shirt and a white tie. Red rose thrust in the buttonhole of his lapel, hat on his head, thick rings cladding his fingers.

'Spiffy, huh? Pretty sharp for your old dad. I took a couple of cues from a guy I saw on a video I was watching earlier, all dressed up and dancing.'

'Hey, I watched that one too. So I guess that makes this a dancing costume?'

Junior weighed his words, careful not to sound like he was talking back.

'Ridiculous.' Dad puffed out his chest. 'In other videos, I've seen guys wear this kind of thing while riding in cars, or having their nails trimmed at the barber shop. And everyone who sees them treats them with respect. Which, if you ask me, makes this the perfect outfit for a father.'

'Okay, but how come you're almost twice as fat as yesterday?'

'You have to be this big, or else a double-breasted suit won't look right,' Dad said, lacking conviction.

Junior decided not to argue. He shut his book. 'I'm making decent progress with deciphering for the day. Honestly, now that I've got the hang of it . . . it's kinda fun.'

'No one's forcing you to enjoy it . . . I wonder if this book's legit, though. Seems there are three kinds of books: ones that are all lies, ones that are half lies and half true, and ones that are true through and through. Hard telling which is which.'

'You got that right. Why is that? Why bother stringing all those words together if the end result is one big lie?'

Father and son pondered the question. This was a persistent mystery to them. Junior in particular was sceptical. They

74

assumed the videos, at least, were telling the truth, but what were they supposed to do if those were lying, too?

'We human beings are complicated creatures.' Dad sighed. This observation, while not exactly helpful, struck him as a pretty cool thing to say.

'I think this book is true, though,' Junior said. 'It even provides a date for everything.'

'Righto! Keen observation, boy. So smart. Like a father, like a son.' Dad beamed. 'You know, I failed to notice that myself. It's hard to tell what aeon most of these books come from.'

'This one's set in nineteenth-century America. I found it on the map. It talks about the War Between the States. But the main character's a woman.'

'Once you're finished deciphering, tell me if they explain why humans ventured into space.'

'I'm not so sure they will, but I'll keep going anyway. This woman just had her heart broken. Look how many pages I still have left though! So maybe there's time yet for her to wind up on a space-ship. I mean, when people get jilted, don't they usually skip town?'

The gifted son spoke with certainty.

'Suppose so . . .' Dad cocked his head.

'You know, like take a trip? You hear a lot of that in songs.'

'I guess so.'

'I kinda want to try getting my heart broken.'

'I think you'd need to be in a relationship . . .'

'What about my sister?'

'Right. Sure, worth a try.'

'First, though, we have to meet up at a dance party, or go on a date or something.'

'Don't get your hopes up. There's only four of us Earthlings left, after all . . . Who else would you invite? The monsters that gambol they beyond the hill they do?'

'Wait, but can't those guys transform so that they look exactly like us? We could make them tons of nice clothes with the replicator. Then they'd have something to wear.'

'They don't have any interest in that kind of thing. The concept of a civilized existence is beyond them. We're lucky they're tame. They won't do us any harm, but they're obviously a different form of life. Who knows what they're thinking? They'd have a lot more fun if they were living in our automated city. But they insist on roughing it. They must prefer it that way.'

Mom poked her head into the room, hair knobbed with curlers.

'You need to talk some sense into that girl . . .'

She wore a bathrobe and held an orange and a glass of milk.

'What's wrong?' asked Dad.

'She's hiding in the closet again.'

'Huh? What's bothering her this time?'

'It's these awful books. Now she's started reading about how daughters hate their moms and love their dads. As if I needed this today.'

Mom shook her head.

'What?' Dad asked, perplexed. 'What's she been reading?'

'*Psychology* or something. What a load of baloney.'

Junior assumed a noble air. 'Don't worry, I'll get her out.'

'Let me do it,' Dad insisted. 'I call the shots around here, see.'

'Yeah, but Dad, what do you know about books?'

Junior left the room.

~

'How long are you going to keep this up? Get out of there right now!'

Mom pounded on the door.

'Go away!' said Sis. 'I'm being rebellious.'

The response was muffled, as if her face was buried in a cushion.

'You've got it wrong, Sis,' Junior said.

'How so?' she asked. 'I'm an adolescent.'

'We're supposed to be going on a picnic!' Mom shrieked. 'Get out this instant!'

'Hush a minute, will you?' Junior pushed Mom aside, but pushed too hard. She tumbled to the floor and bashed her forehead. For a while she lay still. Leaving her like that, Junior crossed his arms.

'Were you reading about the Electra Complex?'

'Yeah,' Sis answered from the closet.

'Did you know that there's a negative Oedipus Complex, too, though?'

'Huh?' Her voice was quiet. 'What's that?'

'It's when you form an attachment to a parent of the same sex.'

'. . . Isn't that the opposite?'

'Exactly. In psychology, for any given case, there's generally another case that constitutes the polar opposite. Though not in every single situation.'

'. . . Really?'

Sis was losing confidence in her position.

'I've read more books than any of us, right?'

No response.

Mom sat up, feeling woozy. She rubbed her forehead for a while. Apparently it wasn't serious. She went over to the replicator.

'Besides, do you realize how bored you're gonna get if you stay cooped up in the closet?'

Junior was changing strategies.

'. . . But . . .'

'You call yourself an adolescent, but that's bogus. This place has a different orbital period than Earth. Not like I've actually done the math, but I bet it's different alright.'

Junior tried to sound as nonchalant as possible.

'How old are you again?' he asked. 'In local years.'

'Um, I guess . . . like seventeen or something?' Sis was earnest, but sounded doubtful. 'I'm not sure though. Sometimes my calendar stops working.'

'Know what you mean. After a week, it's all a blur. I've been trying to pinpoint when it was that human beings invented time. I'm still trying to figure it out, but evidently time was a big deal.'

Junior pulled up a chair and sat. In imitation of his father, he had a smoke. When he ashed on the floor, the robovacuum scurried over.

'Yeah, but that's exactly why I'm doing this.'

Sis fidgeted in the closet.

'Don't you realize?' Junior asked. 'Time is bogus. After 3 p.m. today, for all we know it'll be 7 a.m. four days ago.'

Mom craned her neck at Junior. She was in the process of pulling a bamboo basket from the replicator. 'What are you saying? Time is passing by just fine, thank you very much. We're the ones who need to make sure that we keep on acting normally. Now get your sister out of the closet. Once I've got everything together, we're heading out. This has been on the docket for quite a while.'

'I get it, okay?'

Junior turned around, knitting his brow. Sometimes, it was okay to get upset with your parents. It was a regular occurrence in the dramas on TV.

'Let's talk about time later. Seventeen, huh? That's pretty old to be going through adolescence.'

'. . . So, what am I supposed to do?' she asked reluctantly.

'Well, women in their late teens wash their hair excessively. They stand in front of the mirror, trying on tons of different clothes. Sometimes they go on dates.'

'Is that supposed to be more fun?'

'Yeah, absolutely. Tons of fun.'

'Alright.'

The door slid open from inside. Sis was sitting in the top compartment of the closet, hugging a pillow. Nimbly, she jumped down to the floor.

'Whew, I'm tired. I was in there six whole hours. Mom took forever to notice.'

She reached her arms up high and stretched.

'We were busy, that's all,' said Junior, attempting to console her.

'I try to be rebellious, and our folks don't even notice.'

Just like that, her voice was buoyant.

Mom headed for the kitchen, arms full of picnic fixings.

'What's that woman doing?' asked Sis.

'Making us lunch. And it's a little weird to call your mom *that woman.*'

'It's fine once in a while.'

'If you say so.'

Junior didn't really know himself.

'I'm going to get ready,' Sis said.

His little sister stood before the replicator and punched a series of buttons.

'*INSUFFICIENT VEGETABLE OIL*,' quoth the replicator.

Among the contents of the basket Mom had set beside the machine was a tub of margarine. Sis scraped the tub clean with a knife, emptying it into the hopper.

The processing light flickered. At length, two tubes of lipstick popped from the machine, accompanied by a gentle tone.

'Hey, think it can make some stuff for me, too?' asked junior.

'Sure.'

'Let's see . . . I'll need a comb and some pomade. Or maybe gel instead.'

'Changing your hairstyle?'

'Yeah. Can't decide if I'm gonna spike it up or do a pompadour.'

Junior thought of all the coming-of-age movies he had seen. All the different styles showcased in the bromides. Granted, the movies had a tendency to over-represent the *American Graffiti* look.

'I'll have some pomade.'

'What make?' Sis shot back.

He hadn't thought of that.

'Do I gotta be specific?'

'The devil is in the details. If you care anything about fashion.'

Sis was a stickler for minutiae.

'What kinds are there? I don't know where to start.'

'So for your different brands of product . . . there's Yanagiya, Fiorucci, Lanvin . . .'

Sis was showing off.

'That many kinds?'

'Then there's Nestle, Ajinomoto, Kewpie . . .'

'Gimme one of the good ones.'

Sis manipulated the machine and pulled out a jar of pomade. It had a Kewpie emblem on the lid.

'It's the little things in life that matter.'

'So I hear.'

'I know way more about this kind of thing than you. I read the women's magazines. I even know more about Sunday brunch than Mom. Girls are supposed to eat yogurt and fruit. Oh, and cheesecake.'

'Look at you, acting like a real girl now.' Junior was genuinely impressed. 'Correct me if I'm wrong, but didn't you used to be a boy?'

'Think so. It's all kind of vague. Mom and Dad decided that having one boy and one girl would make for more variety. But the hairstyle and clothes are totally different. It's a real pain. If I was still a boy, I could just copy you.'

Junior thought back to when his sister was a boy. They both wore shorts and chased each other around, playing tag. Mom was adamant that a child with a girlish body should be raised to be a woman. So his little brother became a little sister. Sis seemed fine with it. After dressing as a girl for a while, her body was much softer looking than before. Thanks to no small effort on her part.

'Where's Mom?'

Nothing else to do, Junior paced around the room.

'Isn't she getting dressed?'

'What's taking her so long?'

'Hellooo! When women go out, it takes them a long time to get ready.'

'But all she has to do is change her clothes, comb her hair, and put on a little make-up.'

'That's not the point . . .'

'Well, what else is there?'

'I dunno . . . but Moms have a lot of stuff to do, like all the time.'

Families depend on every member acting out their roles. Junior went back to his room. He lay down on his bed and put on a tape. Pretty soon, he nodded off.

It took Mom two and a half days to get ready.

The four of them left the house carrying baskets and thermoses. What a clear, gorgeous night it was.

'Aren't we driving?'

'Then it wouldn't be a picnic, dummy.'

They strolled along, buildings towering on either side.

It would appear this city had no residents but them. The windows shone a secretive blue. The buildings were dark inside, cloaked in quietude. Far off in the distance, a steady humming could be heard. Automated switches flicking on and off. Following the curving road, the mercury lamps looked like a string of race cars.

'The view is awful over here,' Dad whispered.

'Don't people usually go on picnics to enjoy the scenery?' Sis asked her brother.

'They go to fields and hills and stuff. Places with big trees.'

'But isn't it unsafe to leave the city?'

Mom turned, eyeing them anxiously.

Not a single one of them had any memory of being outside the city, but somehow, they shared an understanding of what the world outside the city looked like.

It ended abruptly. Rather than a gradual thinning of the buildings, there was a stark line at the edge, as if the whole metropolis had been sliced out from somewhere else and plopped down on this planet. Like the family, it came across as woefully isolated. They had no idea when this city came to be. Settlers from Earth had built this settlement, and for one reason or another fled or all but died out, leaving the few perseverant souls from whom they were descended. At least, as Dad would have it.

Outside the city, hills and fields stretched off into the distance, where prowled the blue-black monsters. Thick bristles on their crowns and backs, squat-legged creatures they. Trotting about on their hind legs. Their front legs were brawny; black claws grew from their fingertips. They appeared to be indifferent to the presence of this Earthling clan.

Though none of them had ever seen one of the monsters, they knew how they looked and behaved. Inexplicably. The monsters subsisted on tree nuts and were exceedingly benign. Or perhaps not benign, Dad told them once, so much as indolent. It was unclear whether they were napping or slacking off. Hence, they could not be human. Human beings, he said, were supposed to lead orderly lives. Their family being a prime example.

'Dad,' asked Mom, 'did you read the morning paper?'

'Yeah,' Dad answered solemnly. He was the one who had insisted they read the newspaper, to 'keep up with the Joneses'. A person who neglects to read the news each morning is a bum, like those who fail to pay their cable bill. But then again, they only used the TV to watch tapes. So who cares about the cable bill. It's not like there were any stations anyway. The newspaper, however, was indispensable. The fact that there was no newspaper company was no excuse.

Using articles from magazines and old newspapers, Dad made his own gazette. Each night before bed, he pushed the shuffle button. If he was too punctilious with the selection, it would spoil the surprise. And he made sure to set the postometer accordingly, so that the paper landed in the mailbox at 5 a.m. each morning.

'Anything good?'

Mom had no interest in the news but let on like she cared.

'Price of wheat's gone up.'

'Again? That's the sixth time this month.'

Her response was artificial, and why not? The articles were artificial too. All that mattered was that they went through the motions.

'It plateaued for a while, though.' Dad was being difficult. 'Look, I've been giving it some thought.'

He crossed his arms and watched their son and daughter, who were now a little ways ahead.

'I think it's time we built a house.'

'Why is that? What's wrong with where we're living now?'

'We can't stay there forever. The only plus about that place is that we're settled in. It's been too long already. We need to resist the temptation of perpetual convenience, every corner spick and span. Human beings only grow through hardship. Building a house is a man's life's work.'

'Where will we go?'

Mom figured why not ask. She knew it was ridiculous, but when he got like this, she had to do her best to play along.

'Where? That's why we're here . . . to find the perfect spot.'

She wouldn't dream of living outside the city. Besides, Dad had no clue how to build a house.

'I will avoid a casual approach to life at any cost.' But Dad immediately qualified himself, to smooth things over. 'I simply don't want us to wind up the butt of the joke. When people behave shamefully, their children follow suit. Children only notice when their parents make mistakes. One false move, and pretty soon they're . . . You know, whatever you call it.'

Dad flapped his hand impatiently.

'Delinquents?'

'Right, right. In no time flat. Who knows why, but kids love being delinquent.'

He was emphatic, though not exactly sure what being a delinquent entailed. It sounded like something from the newspaper, but then again, he was the newspaper.

'I blame it on the motorcycles.'

'Damn straight. Great point, Mom. That's the problem. Motorcycles and cars!'

'But they already have both. They made them with the replicator.'

'Hmm, I don't like the sound of this. We'll have to figure out a subtle way of talking sense into them. Discipline is all about taking the right approach.'

They continued down the deserted street.

'How much further?'

Junior produced his comb and ran it through his hair, making a ducktail at the back of his neck. He took care to ensure that the hair met in a vertical line. A solitary bang fell across his forehead. *I got this*, he told himself. *I am the coolest cat.*

Sis wore an evening gown with a lengthy train. The proper attire for going out at night. She knew the deal. She had debated wearing something disco-formal, but it's not like they were going to a disco, so she gave up on that idea. Someday, though, she hoped to see a disco, at least once, but Dad refused to let her go. He called them dens of ill repute. Thanks to him, she never got to go where all the groovy kids were at. Wherever that was.

'Hey, we're not leaving town, are we?' asked Sis.

'Uh, actually, I think we are,' said Junior.

He popped the collar of his button-down shirt, just for show. Maybe he should untuck the front.

'I wish there were an ocean nearby. Seaside highways are so dreamy.'

She was thinking of a scene from one of the videos.

They arrived at a plaza, theatres on all sides. Fountain in the middle. All the lights were out.

'Hey, what happened here? It's usually so spectacular.'

'Late at night, they turn the lights off.'

'What time you think it is?'

'Hard to say,' said Junior. 'Besides, clocks are bogus. I even get the feeling that time flows differently depending on what part of the city you're in.'

He stuffed his hands into his pockets.

'We left early in the evening, though. And we haven't walked for very long.'

'Now that you mention it, yeah.'

Lately, he'd been losing confidence in how to live his life. Some days he had no idea what to do with himself. Especially when time started expanding and contracting. That really screwed him up. Seeing the sun go down while he was still working on his morning coffee was deeply upsetting. If he sat up doing nothing all hours of the night, his parents scolded him, saying night was for sleeping. When he said he wasn't sleepy, they told him to pretend. Anything else would be indecent. He wasn't to be doing anything disgraceful to society.

He had no idea what they meant by 'society'. What did they mean? Whenever he asked, his parents screamed, 'You've got no common sense! At your age, shouldn't you have some common sense already?'

So he waited for his common sense to arrive on its own. He'd been waiting for a while now. No sign of it anywhere.

Junior worried all the time. (Books told him growing up was about agony and doubt. So maybe this was how it was supposed to be.)

He sat down beside his sister.

'Hey, do you think time is made up?'

Sis looked at him.

'Anywhere there's no people,' he said, 'there's no such thing as time. It's something people made up, out of convenience. To impose order on events.'

'What about history? We're trying to find out what really happened. When and how human beings made it here. Don't you want to know what it was like when they first arrived?'

'These days, I'm not sure I really care about that anymore. Feels immaterial.'

'Watch what you're thinking, boy.'

Dad called to him from the bench where he sat.

'Enough. Quit jabbering.' He shook his head. 'You've got it all wrong, son. Why do you think we read books and watch videos? To learn about the way of life of those who came before us. That's why. They offer us a clear example of how to live life right. We must keep on the straight and narrow. If we go astray, we're toasted.'

'I think each person should live life how they like.'

'That's immaturity for you. At your age, you should be going to school, drowning in homework. You should be thankful for being spared that fate ... Though life would be a whole lot easier for me if there were a school around here. And for you too. On Earth, they had something called entrance exams.'

'I know.'

'It would do you good to have an outlet for your youthful vigour. Burning your glory days on tests – ah, that takes me back!' Dad spread his arms theatrically. 'That's what being young is all about! Testing your mettle. The satisfaction of giving it your all. The beauty!'

'You want me to be some kind of clean-cut poster boy?'

'What else is youth good for?'

'No thanks. Sounds pretty lame. Lately, I've been doubting the advisability of giving anything your all.'

'I'm saying this for your own good, son. Your folks would not mislead you. So listen up.'

'Is that why you're having me create a history of Earthlings, in place of sending me to school? Why do you care so much about history and time, anyway?'

'Have you gone rotten, boy? So, you think you can get away with being a delinquent, huh? Bad kids always spout the same blatherskite.'

'Listen to your father. You'll regret this one of these days. It's like the saying goes: there's no use holding a village at the family grave. Once we're dead, it'll be too late.'

'Don't you mean *vigil*?'

'Same difference. You little brat.'

Junior shut his mouth.

He understood the problem, however tenuously. His parents were uncomfortable with playing Earthlings on this foreign planet. In an effort to conceal their discomfort, they obsessively adhered to social customs, codes of behaviour. Since they were unsure of what, exactly, was the best way for an Earthling to behave, they held themselves and their children to impossible ideals. Their pursuit of the history of their ancestors, too, was a function of their desire for peace of mind.

'Are you a bad boy now?' asked Sis. 'Just a few days ago, weren't you a goody two-shoes?'

She asked this sincerely (not as an accusation).

'That's right. I find it pretty odd myself. While Mom was getting ready to go out, I started thinking about time. After two and a half days of thinking, I realized the idea of linear time does no one any good. If all that matters is survival.'

'I only took an hour. Is your head screwed on okay?' Mom, who was wearing a neckerchief for the excursion, shook her head with vigour.

This got Junior thinking. *What if I'm the only one unstuck from time?*

'Hold on, dear. I think that's going too far.'

'You're probably right. I only want our children to be safe. Sometimes I get carried away . . .'

Mom giggled, covering her mouth with her hand. Then she looked up at her family and gave them a command, in a voice honeyed with enthusiasm. 'Forget I said anything. Let's eat.'

The monsters were huddled together, flank to flank, asleep. The cushy undergrowth provided matchless bedding. A sweet smell wafted from the earth, but the sensual aroma of the trees was overpowering. The beasts were fast asleep, without a care.

Except for two.

Eyes open to the night, they pondered time and the liberty of other living things.

The Earthling family chomped their sandwiches in silence. Before they swallowed their first bites, dawn visited the planet.

'Hey, what's going on? This can't be.'

'What did I tell you? Don't forget to bring your watch,' Mom said. 'Who knows what ungodly hour we left the house.'

She nudged Dad with her elbow.

'This can't be happening.'

Dad's jaw dropped.

'Can't? It's happening, alright, clear as day. What now?'

'I don't see why we can't picnic during the day,' said Sis.

She ate her sandwich beatifically.

'Don't point fingers at me,' Mom snapped. 'Your father's the one who picked the time.'

'I wanted it to be like in that movie, *Picnic on the Night*.'

Dad hadn't a leg to stand on.

'Isn't it *Picnic on the Battlefield*?' Junior interjected.

'Don't talk back, you little shit!' Mom said. 'If we wanted to do that, we'd have to march off into a warzone! Do you realize how hard it is to find a proper battle in this day and age? Of course you don't. Because you don't know anything. You're confused.'

Mom was borderline hysterical.

'Isn't there a *Picnic on Nearside*, too?'

Sis looked at the faces of her family members. None of them seemed to know what she was talking about.

'Oh well. Let's go home.'

Dad spoke with much chagrin. They took their leave.

Something scurried by and stole their picnic basket. A girl. She glanced back at them from the entrance to a theatre. Fulgurous eyes and hair of gold had she.

'Hey, what gives!' Dad yelled. 'That's ours.'

'My cutwork napkins are in there!' Mom cried. 'Don't let her get away with that.'

The girl slung the basket over her shoulder and darted off. She was fast. The family pursued.

'Dad gave me those for our anniversary, in a set with the tablecloth. They're priceless.'

Mom wailed as she ran.

Just when they thought they'd lost her, they saw the girl at the next intersection, waiting for them on the corner.

'She not an Earthling be! I'm positive that we're the only actual Earthlings left!'

Dad was out of steam.

'Are there unactual Earthlings? What would that involve?'

'Quiet! This is no time for insubordination.'

'Can't you make more napkins with the replicator?' asked Sis, keeping pace.

'They have sentimental value! They're the only ones in the entire universe!'

Mom was blowing things out of proportion.

This game of tag – running full speed and stopping short, then dashing off again – continued for some time.

'If she's hungry, we would've shared, but this is unforgivable.'

'I bet she's trying to lure us off somewhere.'

In which case, you would think they would've given up on chasing her, but the parents ran like mad. Junior and Sis chased the girl, too, though not without a modicum of glee.

They reached the edge of the city.

The girl atop a gentle hill stood she.

'No one makes a fool outta this family. We'll get you yet!'

'Stop, dear, it's too dangerous.'

The four of them stood their ground, eyes trained on the hilltop.

An elder appeared from the shade of a great tree and stood behind the girl.

'Sorry for your trouble. I hoped to speak with you, but our kind, as a rule, cannot enter the city. Not because we are unable to, but because we hate it there. It's made by human beings for human beings. No place for us.

The elder's speech was stilted, though his voice was soft.

'Give it back!'

Mom was frantic.

'When we are finished, I will return your things. Long we have been watching you. Not with our eyes, but with our minds. Since this is something that you're capable of too, I think you'll understand?'

'We have no clue who you are!'

Dad was flushed with anger.

'Please, hear me out. Once upon a time, we lived in peace. We may not have manufactured or consumed, but our existences were rich. Alas, in any group, there will always be misfits. Some of us began to wonder why they were alive and where they came from. Their thoughts consumed their every moment. Eventually they set off for the city. The city made by denizens of another star, and then abandoned. Once there, they spent their days deliberating about time and history and origins.'

The elder didn't sound the least bit elderly.

'Are you talking about us? Well, you can quit while you're ahead. We're not like you. We were born in this city. Lived here our whole lives!'

Dad was livid.

'So you don't remember. The memory, however, has a tendency to reorganize itself rather conveniently. I figured it was time to set you straight. Which is why we've led you here. Why do you insist on role-playing as Earthlings – or whatever riffraff you purport to be? You can be free, without such pageantries of humankind. A calm existence, unplagued by these anxieties, is within reach.'

'Asshole!'

Dad swelled with malice. His body literally swelled. Violent shockwaves daggered from his person. Foul electricity, filthy purple. The waves crested the hill and zapped the elder and the girl, killing them instantly.

The family had no idea what was going on. They had never suspected their rising tempers could physically kill someone.

'Phew!' Mom pointed. 'Not human after all.'

Two blue-black monsters slumped at the top of the hill.

'Man, what a surprise!'

Junior snickered. When he beheld the faces of his family, he saw three monsters.

A breeze swept the tranquil hillside. The monsters who had posed as a family stood stock still, overtaken with amazement. They could not wrap their heads around what had transpired or why. Feeling stupid, they remembered now that monsters (such as them) were able to take any form. Perhaps they had been so convinced that they were Earthlings they began to look the part.

The wind changed.

Disregarding one another, the monsters loped off, each heading its own way. Leisurely, with no particular place to go, stewards of a new anxiety.

THAT OLD SEASIDE CLUB

Sunlight floods the bay.

Boys and girls sit on benches beneath the canopy of trees lining the walkway, lapping at ice-cream cones. Others cut zigzagging paths down the walkway on their roller skates. Red and white parasols shelter hot dog stands.

I begin whistling, both hands shoved into the pockets of my denim skirt. The low notes blend together. If I try to whistle too hard, I veer off-key. I can't properly separate the notes of fast songs like this, so they end up merging into each other.

Doesn't match my mood, but I change to the blues. This way, you see, it doesn't matter if the tune wobbles a bit – you can still make it to the end.

Oh, each day is such a gift.

I'm having so much fun that I can't hold back my smile.

But what manner of idiot just stands there grinning all the time? So, I sing these songs all day. I've been like this ever since coming here.

A bus pulls up from behind, letting off Emi. She gives a big wave and runs up to me. 'Where you off to?' She smiles, and a warm breeze teases her curly hair. Then, the scent of the sea.

'The Seaside Club.'

'Oh, same here!'

The sign outside of this bar on the outskirts of Yokohama actually reads 'Serenity'. Kind of sounds like somewhere you'd go to 'die with dignity', to be honest, so we've chosen our own name for it. And everyone here just calls this area 'the seafront'. Some folk go for 'coastal promenade', but who knows what they're on about.

Emi and I walk along by the pier, looking at the Hotel New Grand off to the side.

The melody in my head goes on, coming out as a hum now, not a whistle.

'What's that one called?' Emi looks at me.

'Can't say. I'd have to get back around to the hook first.' I'd stopped following the lead guitar to answer her, but I pick it up again straight away. Emi joins in with an organ-like tone. Our jam continues, on and on.

And there's no stopping us, not even now we've reached the Seaside Club. The mood of the piece has become quite melancholy, or serious, but it'd be no fun to cut it off, so we stand there, carrying on. Finally, we find a chance to get back to the hook. She seems to know the song too, and we really get into it. And, like an avalanche (or so we think), we slide into the ending. The End. Or not – I decide it was a pause, and then add one last phrase. If I had a guitar, I'd be playing a trailing solo that lingers through a slow fade before disappearing, like a whistle in the darkness.

'What was it, again?' I ask, pushing open the glass door of the bar.

'"I Can't Keep from Cryin' Sometimes",' Emi answers quietly.

Can't help but cry. True that. But I wonder why a song with a title like that came to mind.

Anyway, we make for the bar stools as usual, without giving the song any further thought.

'It's just beautiful outside,' I say to the bartender.

'It's always like that here. Everyone's so content at first,' he replies, coolly.

'What's that supposed to mean? You can live a life of absolute leisure here.'

I'd won my place in a lottery. The ticket came with some tissue paper I'd idly bought . . . I think. (My days here are like tissue paper too, I suppose – I float around, dazed, and any memories of the past are blurred and hard to pin down.)

'Oh, but you'll tire of that. If you're a committed sort.' This barman likes to get up on his high horse.

'We can stay here as long as we like, can't we? And we're free to go back to Earth any time,' Emi says, fiddling with her paper napkin.

'Technically, I suppose. Do you want to go back?'

'No, no,' she shakes her head, 'I've only been here half a month.'

'Wait!' I turn to her. 'Didn't you say it was half a year, before?'

'I never said that.' She pauses a moment and adds, more sweetly, 'You must've just misheard.'

One wonders. I mean, I've been here around a fortnight, and seeing as she was here before me . . .

'A beer, perhaps?'

'Oh, forgot to order. Yes,' I reply to the barman, 'in a small glass, please.'

He places a delicate fluted glass on the counter, and then a freshly opened bottle. Emi glares as he performs this routine. She's always like this when I drink.

'It's the middle of the day, so . . . I'll have something soft,' she says, slowly.

Emi didn't win any lottery – she's here for therapeutic reasons, a change of scenery. Apparently the air on this planet does you good. She says she's twenty-five years old. I'm not sure what she was doing before coming here.

'Go pick some music,' she says quietly, her mind elsewhere.

Stood beside the jukebox, I touch the screen and begin scrolling down through an endless stream of song names and numbers. There are enough records in this thing to fill an entire radio station's back catalogue. I get sick of sifting through them all, so I just choose three tracks without much thought, and head back to the bar.

'What did you go for?' Emi props her elbows on the bar.

'Some rhythm and blues.'

'Nice.'

A shrill, tinny voice sings 'Lucille' – could be a woman or a young boy. I spend a moment captivated by their strange enunciation, which wraps around the lyrics as if the words were the singer's own. I take a sip of beer and put my glass down again. Emi glares fiercely at my hands.

'My mum, she . . .' After a pause, she breaks the silence, 'She's an alcoholic. Drinks from the morning and right on through. She doesn't care, as long as she has her sauce. And it's not about the taste – she says she never even liked it. But being a little tipsy helps take the edge off her pain, she says.'

The barman listens to her words attentively. Well, I suppose he always takes his job seriously. But once Emi started talking, a slight tension seemed to draw across his face.

'She's always trying to quit, but she winds up reaching for the bottle again. One time, she went to throw away all the booze she'd stored up. Took me with her, too, all ceremonial. And when we got home, she was so happy – "Now I'll never drink again!" – all of that. But just two hours later, she was getting restless. "I should've kept a little drop," she'd say. "Just enough for a little nightcap before bed." And before long she was out buying her bottles again.' She lets out a long sigh, her brows furrowed, and wipes her palms with a tissue pulled from her sleeve.

'And?' I ask, trying to sound as casual as possible, 'Did she ever do anything to you?'

The colour drains from her face. That seems to have unsettled her.

'I'm sorry, I didn't mean . . .' Didn't I? Well, then, what did I mean?

'It's fine, I don't care. You mean, did she hit me, right? Like some drunken guy on a rampage? No, nothing like that. But when my dad left for work, she'd grab a bottle and a glass and head right back to bed. When she was in a bad mood, she'd be like that all day long. Towards the evening, she'd start thinking about preparing dinner – but it's dangerous, isn't it? Cooking when your head's all over the place – spilling, scalding, dropping knives everywhere. So she'd make something up about feeling unwell and go back to bed again.'

Emi wipes her forehead with the tissue.

'Shotgun' plays through the speakers, breaking the silence between the three of us.

'I wonder why I blurted all that out,' she whispers between the phrases in the music.

'Because of this.' I gesture to the beer before me.

'Yeah, that'd be it.'

'I'll never drink in front of you again.'

'Oh no, that's going too far.'

'But it reminds you of your mother, doesn't it?'

'Yeah. It's weird. A little while after I'd arrived here, she started really playing on my mind.'

A door opens and a young barmaid enters the room. The older barman takes off his apron. He only ever works extremely short shifts. I guess it's enough to keep the place ticking over.

'What are you up to tonight?' I change the subject.

The barman begins clearing his things up.

'I'm going to Friday's Angels,' Emi replies, mentioning the name of a kooky nightclub.

'Oh, great idea! Maybe I'll come along.'

It's my kind of place, old-fashioned interior. There's a thickly carpeted floor, raised in bumps here and there for people to sit. And they don't just play the charts – you hear some outrageous tunes in there. The other day they started playing some novelty song called 'Don't Feel like Doing Anything at All', and I couldn't get over it. And there are no kids on the scene.

'And hey, in that case,' Emi adds, 'you might run into Naoshi. He's always there.'

I feel myself blush. The sound of his name alone sets my heart racing.

'He's cute, isn't he?' She laughs. 'Have you spoken to him, at least?'

'Not yet.' I shake my head, bashfully.

'Reckon it'll take a while to get something going?'

The barman adjusts his scarf and leaves. I stare at my hands, gripping my beer glass.

'Well, who knows. Things can shift all of a sudden.'

I found him pretty much straight after I arrived on this planet. He'd come to the spaceport to meet some other girl, as it happened. And, oh, the wariness I felt then, and still now – and yes, that's right. It was wariness, I'm certain. Not excitement.

I'd seen him before, somewhere.

But how?

There's no way I'd ever forget someone so beautiful. And, actually, rather than having *seen* him before, it's like I've been *involved* with him.

'When I first laid eyes on him, I felt like he'd been someone close to me,' I say, absent-mindedly, 'but I also felt this sense of coldness towards my own self; a distance from the version of "me" that had been close to him. It's a weird way of putting it, I know.'

'Hey, how old are you?' Emi sips her lemonade.

'Nineteen.'

'Right. So phrases like "I wanna live again" won't have crossed your lips yet. She used to say that all the time at one point, my mum. "I wanna live again".'

'That was a song, wasn't it?'

'Oh, you can find a song for anything, you know. There's even a song that goes, "This isn't real love, it's just a song".'

Emi grows silent and starts picking at the peanuts set out by the barmaid.

'When did your mum say that?'

'When she was thirty-six. It was a dreadful age for her. All she wanted was to hit reset and start everything over again from twenty-five.'

'Twenty-five? Why so specific?'

'That's how old she was when she got married.'

We fall silent again.

At some point the barman comes back. Music continues playing from the jukebox. Next up is 'Love's End Does You Bad'.

'I'm sorry. I'm all over the place at the moment,' Emi says, after a pause, 'I keep remembering all these things from the past, without meaning to. And these memories – they're so vivid. This stuff about my mum, I mean, it's as though I went through her suffering myself.'

'It's because you've got all this time on your hands.' I play with my silver bracelet. Emi's wearing the same one – they have little discs on them that work as a sort of cash card. While we're on this planet, nothing costs a penny. But neither the barman nor the barmaid wear one.

'You're right. It's so easy to end up imagining stuff when you're idle.'

Seems like she's got her mind on other things today.

A languid song, almost dripping with despair, comes on the jukebox. I check the screen – 'I've Got a Mind to Give Up Living'. Paul Butterfield.

'Can I get you two anything else?' The barmaid asks.

We take the bus out of Yokohama as dusk nears.

'What's the next stop?'

We sit towards the back, and I gaze outside. 'Yokosuka.'

'I want to go shopping,' Emi says, quite out of the blue.

'Shall we get off, then?'

'But we only just got on.'

The sky grows an ever-deeper blue; it's almost too exquisite to watch. I gaze out the window, eyes glued to the view. The sides of the buildings lit by the sinking sun all glow a uniform gold, subtle yet intense. It's as if rectangular shapes have been cut out of the sky, revealing this shining layer beneath.

'I didn't know the city could look like this.'

I feel something drop onto the back of my hand. Tears! Shocked, I turn to face Emi.

'This is the first time I've cried over a little scenery.'

'It seems like everyone starts being honest with themselves about their feelings, once they come here.' She takes a tissue from her pocket and puts it to my nose. 'Well, it's different for the workers, of course.'

She seems troubled. I blow my nose. Come to think of it, this must be the first time since I was a child that I've cried in front of another person.

'Apparently there's something in the air here that gets you all wistful and nostalgic. Hey, are you glad you came?'

'Of course I am!' I answer, ardently.

I haven't told Emi about this yet, but I had absolutely no friends before this year. It was a serious problem – and not one that could be easily explained away by shyness or introversion. I did have an idea of why people didn't like me, but I just wasn't prepared to admit it. I consoled myself by deciding that I hated other people and had no desire to love anyone.

But I'm drawn to Emi now, after only meeting her a couple of times. And there's Naoshi, too.

'We shopping, then?'

'Oh, right.'

'Let's get off here.'

And the magic doesn't wear off, even after we leave the bus. It's actually painful how beautiful even the ground is, and how the air is laced with the sweet scents of spring.

The last of the sunlight gives an even coat to the tops of the buildings. I can see the start of Chinatown a little down the road.

'Ages ago, I used to go out with this boy from Hong Kong. What was his name? Law, something like that.' Whose words are these coming out of my mouth? There's no way that could've happened to me. On Earth, all I did every day was trudge back and forth between class and home. Are these someone else's memories?

'What was he like?'

'Good at looking after money, but I don't mean he was a cheapskate! He was very orderly. And extremely romantic.'

'Hmm, well. Bet he was a pretty randy bastard then, wasn't he? Often the case with those outwardly rigid types.' Emi never ceases to impress me with her insight.

'Yeah, he was! Feels like an age ago now, though.'

'Bet he was always posing, right? And almost *too* protective.'

'Uh . . . Well, he didn't love me much, so I never had the benefit of any protection like that.'

And it was aged twenty-four that I lost myself to Law's almond eyes . . . Just when did I take over someone else's life?

We've arrived at an area lined with brash American-style boutiques.

'You know, I was hoping for something grungier.'

'How about those punky places over there, then?'

I buy a stole made of yellow netting and a rose to wear around my neck. Still not quite there. Then, a black suit from a less racy shop – with a tight skirt, mind, not trousers.

'Want to come round to mine for dinner?' Now, I'm only inviting Emi over because I hate being alone with CHAIR. This is a chair that sits in the middle of my apartment and talks to me – and only ever to say mean things! It's pretty ridiculous for a piece of furniture to have a personality, but that's just how it is. And it talks just like my mother.

'I'm kind of tired. It's been an intense day. I want to take a break and digest it all, by myself.'

The fact is I've had my fill of her already, so I'm secretly quite glad. But where's my sense of agency? It makes me sick, seeing myself so limp-willed.

Emi raises her hand in the darkening blue light, and I sigh as she turns and walks away, as though the words 'free will' were written across her back.

~

Once I get home, I take tonight's clothes out of my wardrobe and lay them on the bed.

I sit down beside them and light a cigarette, and CHAIR pipes up. 'What about the new outfit?'

'Oh, the black one?' I lay out the black suit, too.

'Why did you go and buy that?' She has a rough, raspy voice, husky yet piercing – she sounds just like my mother, and I hate it.

'I thought maybe Naoshi could be into plain girls. And it makes a statement, doesn't it?'

'Do you know why you've become so obsessed with that boy without even having spoken to him yet, by the way?'

'Because he's bloody gorgeous, right.'

'Wrong!' CHAIR gives an evil cackle. 'You already know him, child.'

She shakes with laughter, her balding velvet cover trembling with its greyish floral pattern, and her armrests wobbling, too.

Now, I've never sat on this chair – she started jabbering away at me the day I took this room. Anyway, you can tell her springs are probably broken just by looking at her.

'Look, Naoshi is someone you used to know. That much is true.' She takes a few steps to the side.

'Why did I forget him, then?'

'Because your long string of failures begins when things start going to pot with him. It takes you a whole decade to even realize he's serious about you.'

'Does he dump me?'

'No, child.' CHAIR strides about the room.

'So . . . You mean there's some misunderstanding between us and we split up. Is that it? I mean, there's no way I'd be the one to leave him.'

'What if you are?' She lets out a snigger.

'No, I'd never –'

'Oh, come on, I just wanted to scare you a bit!'

'But, look – that's not something that happens to this "me", here, right? It's not *me* that makes that mistake.'

'Well, I suppose we could say so,' CHAIR says with a speculative air, before shimmying back to her original spot.

'That's something done by another "me", in a parallel world, right? How old am I there now?'

I realize it's a stupid question as soon as I've said it. Which 'now'? How do you even define that?

'You're in your thirties, probably. You've realized your mistakes and you're stuck in a whirlpool of despair. You're in a state, like that last song you put on at the Seaside Club. Seems like you've actually gone a bit mad.'

'Oh, cheers.'

'No need to thank me, dear.'

'I seem to be wrong in the head here, too.'

'How come?'

'I mean, a chair's talking to me.'

'You get doors and microwaves that talk, don't you?'

'That's because someone's made them that way!'

It's gone seven o'clock.

Cooking can be a pain when I'm on my own. (CHAIR doesn't eat anything, you see.) And my diet is horrific. I suppose I hate fresh fruit and veg because my mum was always telling me to get my five-a-day in. She'd always be saying, 'It's good for your looks. Ugly girls need all the help they can get!'

So, three pieces of stale cake it is – straight in my gob.

'Aren't you going out?' She knows everything.

I take a bath, which makes me sleepy. I put my pyjamas on and lie in bed. The clock by my bedside reads a little before eight.

'Get dressed, do your make-up!'

'I'm shattered. Be quiet for a bit.'

'You're scared, aren't you? That's what it's really about. You're worried you'll mess it up again.' I hear mockery in her voice.

'Sure, maybe. But why did it happen before?'

'Because you had no self-confidence. Naoshi's always surrounded by girls, looking bored, right? And you were just too damn proud to let anyone know how that made you feel. You hid it from him. Never even occurred to you that he might doubt himself too.'

'What did you say?' I ask, leaping up.

I'd heard CHAIR's words, though – we both know that. So she says nothing more.

It's way past eight o'clock.

Emi must've left by now. I consider calling her . . . But only *consider*. I don't actually do it.

'How long are you planning on staying on this planet?' asks CHAIR after about half an hour has passed.

'I want to stay here forever.'

'Everyone says that, dear. But you can't, can you? You have to live your life. You have to cook, clean, look after the kids when they're sick. You have to go out to work.'

'Why do I have to keep on living that life?'

'Well, I'm not sure why.' Her voice strikes a gentler chord, all of a sudden.

And I repeat that phrase in my head. 'I'm not sure why.' I fluff my pillow, turn off the lights, and chant a spell. *Sleep, sleep.* Make the world disappear.

Two days later, and I've made it to Friday's Angels. 'Heroin' is playing, which is a major plus – but no sign of Naoshi.

'Apparently he was *just* here,' Emi yells. You have to shout to be heard. 'He came in with that girl there,' she says, pointing to a blonde dancing centre stage. A different girl to the one he was with at the spaceport.

I go to the bar and order a 7Up.

There's a strobe light pulsing, and people's movements skip between each flicker. It could be a time-lapse video, with a fresh troupe of frozen corpses searing every flash-lit frame.

The lighting becomes more psychedelic. I cut through the middle of the dance floor (keen to get a good look at this blonde) and make for the door. Not particularly pretty. (Not that I'm *particularly* pretty, either.)

Naoshi's there, sitting on the stairs.

'Aren't you coming inside?' I ask, standing still.

He keeps his head down and says something back. I don't hear him.

'What?'

He repeats himself, but the sound coming from inside the club swallows his words, and I can't make out what he's saying.

I sit down beside him. He's repeating, I think, the same words again, and with great patience.

'This girl said she wanted to come, so along I came . . . But I just hate people looking at me.'

I say nothing.

Apparently he came to this planet around the same time Emi did, whenever that was. And he's famous, so I knew his name straight away.

He cuts a very striking figure and there's a distinct aura about him. Some would say he has a sort of ethereal beauty, and you can't help but know he's only half human.

He was one of the first alien 'blends' and, well, his almost completely green head of hair is hard to overlook.

Expressionless and gloomy, he has these severe, empty eyes that seem to say he's long given up on any kind of hope or ambition.

I take a sip from my bottle and pass it to him. He looks back at me with that wide, unsettling stare – it's like looking into the glass eyes of a creepy doll. His eyebrows are also a deep green and bushy around the sockets.

Meekly, he sips the 7Up.

'I don't get it. Girls always want to come to these crowded places. I just wanted us to be alone together, somewhere quiet.'

'Well, it's because they want to show you off.'

He runs his long fingers through his hair.

I can hear some popular song playing through the door. The dry superficial performance sounds pretty funny to me now. The melody is so monotonous, and the phrases are excessively long. Grand old golden-ratio tunes just don't seem to suit this era.

'You know, lately,' I begin, slowly, 'I'm finding it hard to identify what happiness and pleasure *are*.'

He looks up.

'Well . . . Does it matter? If something feels good, that's pleasure.' He gives a weak laugh. 'Nothing more to it.'

'Seems like you live a pretty straightforward life.'

'Oh, I've got my problems. You know, I used to comb over and pick apart *every* single day. Then, all of a sudden, I stopped thinking – I became ill . . . My brain cells took some damage, and I lost the ability to, I dunno, think like I used to.'

It's as if he's talking about someone else entirely.

'What do you mean, you're ill?'

'I'm a drug addict.'

He looks up at me after giving this blunt answer, trying to gauge my reaction. I fight the muscles in my face, trying to keep from expressing anything.

He gets up.

I follow his line of sight to find a boy standing at the bottom of the stairs, seemingly fixed to the spot, looking like a glitch in the scene. He's an absolute fashion victim, with a bandana tied around his calf. Brilliant. Doesn't suit him at all, sadly.

The boy makes his careful way up the stairs, step by step. He's smaller than Naoshi height-wise, but sure makes up for it in width. One of those baby gym-rat types.

'Need to have a word with you, pal,' the boy says, with a cracked voice.

Here we go, I think to myself.

'I don't think I know you,' Naoshi says, apparently racking his brains.

'About the girl.' He glares at me. 'Her, there.'

'Sorry, *what*?' I step closer.

'Don't be moving on other people's girls, you hear me?' He looks at us both.

'Since when am I *your* girl?'

'Look, there's no sense in pretending. We met twice before, out there, and you made them moves on me, remember? "The world's gonna end soon," you were saying. "Let's watch it go, together." And I've been preparing for it! But here you are, spilling all the fucking beans to this one.'

'He's a nutcase!' I say.

Naoshi lets out a long sigh. 'Everyone's messed up here.'

The boy tries to grab my arm.

He falls down the stairs. Naoshi yells something. The boy hits the landing hard.

Seems I'd kicked him over with my very own boot. I say 'seems', because my body moved before I'd even thought about it. I stand very still, surprised by my own actions. 'Is he knocked out?'

Naoshi is intolerably calm. 'It's fine. He didn't hit his head.'

The boy gets up, clumsily, trying to recover his dignity.

Emi comes out through the door. 'Fancy getting something to eat? Oh, dear. That blonde girl's looking for you, you know.'

Naoshi makes to leave, but pauses and asks me, timidly, 'Mind if I come see you tomorrow?'

'What time?'

'Just after noon.' And he heads indoors before I can even nod my head.

I lean against the wall. 'I wish he'd stop this.'

'The fighting?'

'No, no, that was me. That's not what I mean.'

'You're shaking.' Emi gives me a hug.

I open my mouth to say something, but close it again.

'Let's go.' She leads us out, and as we approach the landing, the muscly boy is still there, staring dumbly at me.

Cloud covers the night sky.

We walk along, blown by a warm and balmy breeze.

Wide streets, dark buildings – now and then, a peaceful haze will soften the neon lights of the drive-ins and the night-club doors.

'Doesn't this town make you feel all nostalgic?' Emi voices what I'd been thinking. 'You know, I'd always assumed I just wasn't capable of seeing myself with real emotional clarity.'

'Well, without that clarity, you'll never make it to the big leagues. You'll just spend your whole life stuck among the amateurs.'

We cross the bridge. Chains of boats line the river. The road by the edge seems to be part of some big construction project, with cranes overhead casting their dinosaur-shaped shadows. The lights of cars following the curves of a distant motorway are joined like a necklace.

A desolate scene, quite apart from the seafront. Yet I still feel a similar sense of nostalgia.

'But recently, you know, I've been having these moments of shining coherence. I really mean it.'

'So until now you've just been laying on emotion for show when you're with other people?'

'I suppose so. Hey, how about that place over there with the orange curtains?'

It's an all-night cafe with poky windows, a cheap air and a sparse scattering of customers.

Emi and I sit at a table by the wall, and a waiter approaches with a lengthy menu. Can't be bothered with that, so we just go for the set meal and drink.

'What've you been seeing so clearly now, then? People say all sorts of things, don't they, like: "I'm turning into my mother," or "I'm really feeding the weak woman stereotype".'

'There's not much difference really, is there?' Emi's mouth creases into a smile. 'Everyone thinks they're unique when they have these moments of clarity. Kind of like how you felt when you cried in Yokohama, perhaps. I don't know. I find those moments allow me to forgive myself, even if it's just a little bit . . . And I forgive my mother, too.'

'Things gets easier once you acknowledge the situation.'

'That's right. Even if you don't solve anything. It's the same with my own illness, too. It might flare up again once I've gone back to my life on Earth. It might not. There's no controlling that. It's not a good habit, to want to solve everything.' Emi gazes elsewhere as she speaks.

My meal arrives. There's the main dish, a salad, and also a small glass of rosé.

'Is this included? It wasn't on the menu.'

Emi wraps her handkerchief round her finger. Before long, her order comes too. And, sure enough, another glass of wine.

'They're really testing me.' The handkerchief, tied like a rope, turns her finger white.

114

'Come on, it's fine—' I begin, only to be shocked by Emi's intense glare, seething with energy. I thought her gaze would pierce right through the glass. She looks away and wraps the handkerchief tighter, until it hurts. Her hands are shaking.

'Hang on, was that . . .'

She looks up. Resentment wells in her eyes and spills out with her tears. 'That's right. The stuff about my mum – that's *me*. And no, I didn't mean to lie about it. I just couldn't acknowledge that part of myself. It was too painful, so it had to be smuggled in under the guise of my "mother." They put us to sleep before we came to this planet, right? They must've manipulated our minds along the way, somehow.'

I stand up, shuffle round the table, and sit down next to Emi. Though they're both types of addict, there's a stark difference between an alcoholic and a dope fiend. The boozer clearly needs other people. They're clingier than junkies. Now, if you're hooked on tranquillisers or painkillers, you may be less bother because you become so passive, but you'll inevitably be cold, distant and unfeeling.

But how do I know all this?

Emi continues sobbing.

'You know, I'm not sad at all. I did just realize that this alcoholic mother of mine is me. But these tears, they aren't because I'm *sad*.'

I grab my bag and pull out a handkerchief. Emi uses her own to blow her nose, then thanks me and reaches for the new one.

'Do you mind?'

'Not at all.'

Her tears subside. She dabs at her eyes and tries hard to smile. 'Feels good to cry.'

'Yeah.'

'I'm going back to Earth tomorrow. That's my illness: I'm an alcoholic. I think I'll make it through.'

'Wait, hold on! Tomorrow, that's—'

'The sooner the better. Let the Seaside Club barman know, will you? He's been a great help.'

I've come to depend quite heavily on Emi, so I feel a bit dejected. She knows what I'm like. You end up completely hooked on people who indulge you. Naoshi, though – he hardly seems the dependable type.

'We'll meet again, I know it.'

I listen to her words, crestfallen. I stare at those glasses of wine, as if they harboured destiny itself.

I can't have slept more than a few minutes before a faint knock wakes me up.

'The sun's barely up, you know,' whispers CHAIR.

I go to the door in my pyjamas, barefoot. There's no intercom.

And there stands Naoshi. He stretches his long neck, his hair covering his eyes. 'I thought you might be out,' he smiles faintly, with his big lips.

'Why?'

''Cause it's so early in the morning.'

I really don't see his point. He smiles again. It's a bit of a grimace, actually – he seems slightly unhinged. Exhausted, too.

'Come in.'

He moves to the sofa.

'How did you know where I live?'

'I just ran into Emi. She had a suitcase with her. Pretty thing.'

'Have you been up all night?'

'Don't worry, I'll go home soon.'

'Do you want tea or coffee? I've got jasmine tea, too.'

He lays on the sofa, his eyes on my bare legs. Then, a moment later: 'Coffee's not very good for you, you know.'

'Says the drug addict.' I put the kettle on.

'I'm sick of these reboots,' he murmurs, facing me, as I open the can of jasmine tea. 'I've had so many already, redoing things over and over again.' I can see only his green hair from the kitchen. 'This is maybe my fourth time coming here.'

I take the mugs out of the cupboard.

'Correct,' announces CHAIR.

I almost drop the mugs.

'This isn't about "redoing things". There's no starting over,' she says. 'You go through some similar experiences every time – it's about letting go, basically.'

I cower at CHAIR's shrill voice, but Naoshi doesn't seem bothered by it at all.

I quiver as I make the tea.

'Reboots are about letting go, and accepting things,' CHAIR emphasizes, more quietly.

Naoshi opens those cold, unsettling eyes and watches me settle his mug on the table. He sits up and lets out a sigh long enough to carry his whole soul.

'You're growing on me,' he says offhand, with a shrug of his thick eyebrows, 'I've come to like you now, having met you so many times here on this planet.'

'Here he goes, blabbing on again.' More mockery from CHAIR.

'It's simple really. So this is my fourth reboot. Now, for some reason you didn't turn up on my third – I guess they try mix it up a bit.' I don't think he can hear my speaking furniture. 'Well, it's made me believe in fate anyway. I always end up the same no matter what path I take.'

'Can you time-travel, is that what you're on about?'

'Nope.' He shakes his head.

I sit on the bed, drinking my tea.

'And if you really think about it,' Naoshi says to himself, 'it's not so bad.'

'No thinking needed,' quips CHAIR.

'You know,' I say, 'I thought you'd be more introverted, a man of fewer words.'

'I am, when I'm out there. And I'm pretty loaded right now, too.'

I get up and sit by his feet. 'Hey, what exactly are these "reboots" all about?'

'It'll become clear, soon enough,' he replies quietly, sounding a little weary.

'Now then, look at this old scene,' CHAIR begins, 'you're hoping to get him to say he likes you again, aren't you? But you needn't bother. He could say it a hundred times and you'd still never be satisfied. Not even a thousand times would work. And it's because, child, you just don't love him. Not one bit!'

118

The nerve of this chair, using a word like 'love'? Has she no shame?

All the same, I get my sweet and coy act on (tilting my head to one side, etc.) and ask him, 'What's love?'

'This, surely?' He reaches out and places his hand on my shorts, on my crotch, before immediately taking it away again. He did it so casually I couldn't even jump. 'I'm a horribly direct guy, aren't I?'

Oh, but if I showed some force, he'd bend to my will. You see, Naoshi had long ago disembarked from his life, had withdrawn and shut himself away in this pillowy narcosis. And now, he's merely watching himself drift on – watching, wholly numbed, and without emotion. I doubt he could even muster the energy to try and understand anyone else. In that head of his, there probably isn't much difference between me and his old guitar. And he isn't trying to hurt anyone – no, not at all. He's just . . . checked out.

But who cares if he objectifies us? It's all fine with me.

'Well, he's not exactly "fine",' CHAIR says, *in my head.*

I want to make him mine.

'And you reckon you'll bring an end to your endless string of failures that way?'

I know, I know. But the reason I want him is something more urgent than love.

To me, you see, Naoshi is . . . *a symbol of a certain time.* And the voice in my head is no longer CHAIR's. A *make-believe time. I made it up, all by myself.*

'Mind if I stay here a bit longer?' He seems more relaxed all of a sudden. And then I remember. He asked the same thing

119

before. Back when I was twenty years old. An endless age had passed since then.

'Why don't you sleep in the bed?'

'Okay.' He begins taking off his clothes.

I open the curtains slightly to look outside. A new day – fresh, luminous – is already starting. I imagine I'll head back to Earth eventually. Once I manage to let go completely. I no longer care about happiness or unhappiness. I just hope the scenery's pretty, wherever I am.

'Aren't you going to lie down, too?' Naoshi calls out to me from the bed. I lift up the covers and get in beside him.

He wraps his arms around my neck. And he speaks now, in a gentle voice, to no one in particular. 'Don't worry. The world won't stop spinning. It'll keep going, even if you don't want it to. On and on, until you're absolutely sick of it.'

The barman from the Seaside Club is staring into my eyes when I wake up.

'How're you feeling?'

'Not too bad.'

He's a doctor, and we're on Earth.

'You didn't get what you were looking for, though.'

What a serious look on his face!

'I've come to accept that it just might not be possible.'

I can see a dull-coloured sky through an open curtain. Weak sunlight is coming through the window.

'That planet isn't real, is it?'

'That's correct. Everything you experience there has been programmed and transmitted to your brain. We didn't want to create a fantasy world, you know, where everything's just as the patient wants it.'

'What if they never want to come back?'

'We forcefully wake them up, which can be quite painful, psychologically.'

'And the travellers with silver bracelets were all patients, weren't they? So everyone else must've been fabricated, imagined . . .'

'Emi, who we discharged a little earlier – she left her contact details. Seems she wants to meet up with you.'

She must be thirty-six years old, in this world. Naoshi must be out of the facility too, then. He took off from that planet three days earlier.

I get up.

No need to look in a mirror. I already know the score: I'm a dejected housewife, in my thirties – impatient and frustrated, yet too limp and lethargic to do anything about it. And I live in one of those hideous, uniform, low-rent apartments I can see out the window.

The doctor has left.

I change into my clothes.

Waiting for me in the corridor is my husband.

Naoshi's grown so shabby and unsightly, a goblin next to his past self. Silently, he steps towards me.

I take his hand, for the first time in forever. 'Please, let's not go to that planet anymore. Do you realize what these reboots are doing to us?'

He issues some vague sounds in response.

And outside, the day turns to a swampy night.

SMOKE GETS IN YOUR EYES

I was just killing time. After I had cleaned my room, cooked, and finished the dishes, I had nothing left to do. So I was hanging around at this arcade, you know? I was there by myself.

I became aware of someone approaching me from behind. It wasn't like a shadow fell over my game, but I'm sensitive to these things. It seemed like the person was standing and watching me. I looked over my shoulder, wanting to know who it was.

I saw an older woman, probably a little over sixty. She was filthy, her hair in disarray. She was wearing a jacket that looked like a potato sack. Did she work here?

'Are you winning?' The old woman smiled and immediately her face turned into a topographical map of a mountain range. What? What does she want?

'I'll give you these.' The old lady brought out a handful of tokens from her pocket.

'Oh! That's so kind of you.' As usual, I went along with it. I'm very good at going along with people. When I was a kid, Gran would call me a sycophant.

'But, are you sure?' I asked drawlingly.

She didn't say anything and smiled slightly. A very deep dimple appeared next to her lips. It was disturbingly erotic. I got goosebumps. I couldn't tell if it was a pleasant or unpleasant feeling. What was going on here? This old woman's dimple was far more affecting than a young girl's. Was I actually a pervert? I knew this nineteen-year-old guy who said he was only interested in women younger than six or older than sixty – a sentiment I couldn't understand. Was this how he felt? Anyway, I thought I'd seen her before.

'We've met before, right?' I asked carelessly.

'Sure.'

The old lady was no longer smiling. Was she from my neighbourhood? The people who lived on my floor were mainly all single guys, and she probably wasn't a friend of the old landlady. No matter how much I thought about it, I couldn't recall knowing any babies or old women. My mum was still in her forties, my gran is already dead and none of my other relatives is that age either.

I continued playing the game for a couple more minutes, trying to get these ideas out of my head and hoping she'd disappear. But the old lady didn't make to leave, and I had to stop playing because I have a hard time ignoring people. I get too self-conscious.

Her face looked serious. If I wasn't mistaken, her eyes had a determined look.

Uh, perhaps she's taken a liking to me. That's not good.

'Um, what . . .?' I began asking timidly.

'You forget so easily,' she said in a low, soft voice. And suddenly I remembered – Reiko! I dated her for a bit, when I was twenty and she was thirty-one. Whatever became of her? There was a while back then when I was really worried.

But this old woman couldn't be Reiko. She looked a lot like her, though, so maybe she was her mother. I guess my expression changed because the old woman nodded.

'Want to go get a slice of cheesecake?' She was acting awfully familiar. I wondered if it was a trap. Would I be taken captive by this woman and interrogated about Reiko? The guilty feelings from back then started to revive in me. I couldn't help it.

'Maybe next time. I have work.' I surprised even myself by how smoothly the lie came out.

'You're sure?' That way she raised her eyebrows looked *just* like Reiko. It was rare to find a mother and child who looked so alike. Was Reiko a virgin birth? I remember hearing about that in middle school biology. Apparently, if an ovum is stimulated for some reason and begins to divide its cells, a child can be made with no need for a man. In these instances, the child is always female and will be the spitting image of the mother. I mean, could that be true? Pretty dubious. That teacher was probably spouting whatever came into his head.

'Um, I'm leaving, so . . .,' I put the tokens back into her hand. She was staring at me rather intensely. Something wasn't right. I swiftly left the scene.

I went into a small glass-walled room. This is where I wait in case a machine breaks or somebody has a complaint. That's my job these days.

I took out a cigarette and lit it. No red light was on, calling for me.

Maybe he didn't know who I was. Jane hadn't changed much in three years. But I've aged so much. About thirty years' worth. My body is aging for real. An unbelievable amount. Sometimes when I decide to put on some foundation, to my dismay it gathers around my wrinkles; no matter how well I try to apply it, the foundation just ends up outlining them. The thicker I try to lather it on, the more vivid the lines become and reveal a pattern.

Even I can't believe just how bad it is.

This isn't the kind of place that would hire me. They probably hired me because I'm in my thirties according to my birth certificate. On my résumé, I only wrote in the silver ID number we all have below our clavicles, neglecting to mention the fact that my psychologist had given me *that* treatment. I've already cashed my first weekly pay cheque, but I'm sure they'll wise up soon enough. Could be any day now. What'll I do if I get fired?

There is no day or night here. Boys and girls wearing fluttery clothes come in hordes and all play alone.

Time might begin to pass at a frightening pace again. It's why I incessantly keep checking the clock on the wall. But maybe you could say it would be good for time to pass that quickly again, because I'd age further. Aging is the only way I can imagine dying. Any other way is too scary. I'm terribly afraid of death.

The background music had played all the way through, so I inserted a different tape. What is this? A familiar old song. 'Love's TPO' by Chikada Haruo and Haruophone – I listened to it a long time ago with Jane. I'm sure it was more about affairs or games or free love than romance. It's about a guy with no remorse, who can bring tears to his eyes when he wants to fool a girl.

Nothing needed my attention.

By evening, I had smoked two full packs of cigarettes, doing nothing but listening to music. My eyes hurt. Either from smoking too much or aging too much. Wiping away the tears with the back of my hand, I took the subway out of that level.

I walked for a little while, till I was well off the beaten path. Dingy shops and stalls lined the street. I went into one of them. The old man running the place looked over at me coldly. I took a seat on an unsteady wooden chair and ordered.

Next to me were two young guys sitting side by side. Both were very different from the kind of men who came to the arcade. Those boys have their hair partially dyed or glitter tape wrapped around themselves. They're more like dolls than living creatures. The guys here smelled of sweat. They had lines on their foreheads.

'They have lax security,' one of them was saying. He'd had a bit to drink. 'We do four or five of them and then get the hell out of there. Won't take more than five minutes.'

'You're so small-time. Going after vending machines.'

'It's a pretty promising score.'

'People are gonna notice us, dressed like this.'

'That's no problem. Just cut your hair into a weird shape and then fix a ribbon to the hem of your trousers.'

'I've been wearing the same trousers for three weeks now. They're pretty grimy.'

A dirty night was falling.

I paid and left. A cheap apartment complex halfway up the winding hill is my current abode. When I took my shoes off at the entrance, I found a hole in the sole. That'd be why my feet kept getting dirty.

Chaotic doesn't even begin to describe my room. The last time I cleaned was four months ago, after all. Magazines I picked out of the rubbish bin in the terminal were scattered around. The only light comes from the double-ringed fluorescent bulb that hangs unadorned from the ceiling. There's no lighting on the walls. I leave the place lit up when I go out because it's lonely to come home by myself at night. Besides if I walk into this room with the lights off, I'll definitely trip over something.

When I took my clothes off, I saw the side wrinkles on my stomach drooping downwards. There were lots of them. I tried pinching. Gross. It looked like the edge of a pile of futons. I hadn't thought my body was *this* sickening.

Because I had aged so rapidly, I wasn't used to it. It made me question if this was really me, really my body. I still hadn't quite accepted it.

It was six months after my third divorce. I was working as a part-timer at a jazz cafe and bar. Every other day, I worked from noon to eleven at night. I had just started the job.

'What's that guy of yours doing?' The manager of the bar poured herself a glass of Cinzano. Who was she talking about?

'Well, aren't you something . . . Getting married so many times. Can't you do anything else?' one of the customers chimed in. The counter seats at this place always drew a rowdy crowd. The quiet ones tended to sit in the booths.

'I know, right? Me, I'm just not the family type. It took me ten years to realize that. I'm already thirty-one.'

'Have you ever thought that the problem might be the people you choose?' a different customer asked.

'I can't seem to say no when someone pursues me. It's my fault for always being drawn to unstable people.' I started washing the dishes.

'You're not going to dance anymore?' This one knew my history. I'd been a chorus girl before my first marriage.

'It's been too long.'

A slight pain ran through me. I'd loved dancing ever since I'd been a kid. When I was in middle school, I could often be found making up my own moves and dancing by myself in the gymnasium after school. You couldn't call it modern dance or jazz ballet. I didn't care what it was, I just moved around to the music that I heard in the moment. I didn't have any ballet shoes but I would dance till my toenails cracked and bled.

'Listen, that kind of dancing isn't about talent. That's not so important. It's all about whether you're beautiful or not.'

That long-time dream of mine had crumbled away years ago. I just didn't want to accept that then.

'You're still beautiful,' the bar manager said. She seemed to have a soft spot for me for no discernible reason. I'm sure she found it strange herself, but anyway I got a lot of dresses and accessories out of her.

'You been doing those drugs? You really shouldn't, you know.'

'I'm still doing them.' My voice was low and clear. My medication had been labelled a narcotic and controlled substance a couple of years ago. I'd taken to paying my pharmacist friend to sell it to me under the table.

'I hear the side effects are horrific. If you do too much, your body starts to fall apart and you age much faster than the average person.'

But *those* drugs were good. My anxiety would disappear. When I was so bored I could die, it made time feel shorter. It could even go the other way around.

Those drugs may have caused my last divorce – no, I started taking them because things weren't going well already. Which was it? Not that it mattered either way.

The door opened and a boy walked in. His hair was long and he had a girlish face. He was so skinny that his horrendous pink shirt with yellow polka dots hung like a dress on him. Wow, he's just my type, I thought. I can't help having bad taste. Girls have weird taste these days. And the only people who have the hots for manly men tend to be mainstream homosexuals.

'Been a while,' the manager said.

He ordered a beer in high spirits.

'This must be Reiko!' he exclaimed as he sat down on the stool in front of me.

'That's right. The one who used to dance.' The manager didn't seem to like this one much.

'I know. I used to admire her,' he purred.

When I popped a cigarette into my mouth, he lit it for me. That was ten years ago, I thought, there's no way he'd have seen me dance. He would have been in primary school then.

'I was mature for my age,' he said, reading my bemusement.

When I moved my fingers in an odd way, he gave me his handkerchief. This guy is hyper-attentive, I thought. My palms were sweaty from the drugs. Back then, I was washing my hands more than twenty times a day.

The conversation continued, with no new orders.

I felt slightly nauseous so I went to the bathroom. My stomach was shot. I didn't know if it was because of my recent insomnia or the drugs. Shaking, I threw up a little. When I raised my face, it looked greenish. I was so horribly nearsighted that my features looked blurry. I knew that my skin was in bad shape, though. I pulled out my compact and powdered my nose.

I was still feeling rather queasy when I got back behind the counter. When I squeezed my wrist, he said, 'Let's see,' and felt my pulse.

'Wha – that can't be right.' He tried again. It wasn't a mistake. 'That's gotta be one-forty.'

I nodded.

'Isn't a normal pulse sixty to eighty per minute?'

To change the subject, I said, 'Oh, I dig this sound. It's pretty good.' The manager held back her laughter and pointed at the record cover. What was 'pretty good' was John Coltrane's *A Love Supreme*. Something must be wrong with my head.

I did something like that again later that night. 'I hear this one a lot. What's it called again?'

'Um, it's probably a very famous song,' he said, continuing to smile. The guy's brightness felt slightly fake. Too much need to please.

'Yup. It's famous alright. Dolphy's *Last Date*.' The manager paused. 'You don't look well,' she said, sticking out her chin.

'My head doesn't feel good,' I said in a monotone.

'I'll take you home then. I know I sound innocent but maybe my ulterior motive is to take you somewhere dark,' he said.

He showed a lot of gum when he laughed.

In my dreams, he appeared as a woman named Jane. When I awoke, I found him staring at me intensely. His eyes were unnecessarily big – it was horrifying. When I rolled over in bed, he put on a forced smile. He picked up a hairbrush.

'I'll brush your hair for you. I'm really good at doing things like this. I can do any kind of housework, too. I'm way handier than most women. It's like . . . I can survive by myself. I'm the kind of guy who never need get married.' He kept yapping on about things he couldn't care less about. Jane sometimes fell into a hole all by himself. Whenever he caught me silently looking at him, he would immediately start to clamber out and get all excited. It was hard to figure out what he was actually thinking.

'You're beautiful,' I said as he teased my hair.

'No way! I really hate my face. It's too smiley.'

'But you're ugly on the inside.'

Jane's head was tilted away from me as he tried to brush my hair on one side, so I couldn't make out his expression.

'Maybe it's because I'm two-faced? Been this way since I was a child. I don't trust others, you know. I tell myself there's no way that anybody will ever like me. As a result, even though I'm craving some love, I can never accept it. You know? It's like someone starving to death but not eating the food in front of them because they can't stop wondering if there's poison in it.' When he put the brush back down, his face became expressionless.

'You're afraid of other people?'

'Yeah, it's never turned out well. I have no close friends. Friends are to be used. I'm very good at pandering to others, though.' A feeble smile remained glued to his face.

'I want to do something about that.'

'You shouldn't think like that. It's best to leave people like me alone. We prefer it that way.' The smile had completely disappeared. 'I didn't want to get into this kind of relationship with you. I wouldn't have let things get so far if I'd known you were serious. Now it's . . . different than with the other girls. That's a problem.'

'What are your relationships usually like?'

'Totally throwaway. I anticipate the break-up and hint towards it to prepare for a smooth exit.'

'What happens to you afterwards?'

'Nothing, really.'

I sighed and put my hand in my bag, reaching for my pill box.

'Again?' His eyebrows knitted together.

'Yeah, I . . . can't.' I stood up, poured myself some water and gulped down a bunch in several rounds.

'Why so much? I feel . . . responsible.'

'It's not like you'll do anything about it.'

'Yeah, that's why.'

'You're emotionally stingy.'

'I wonder why that might be.' He said it like he was talking about someone else.

The sun was starting to set. The two of us sat staring at each other in the dimming room, without turning on the lights.

'What happens when you take them? Is it like marijuana?'

'I had this one crazy experience smoking pot. It felt like I was being reborn alongside the birth of the universe. Even when I was aware of talking to someone, five minutes felt like a hundred years. It's rare to get an experience like that. Usually, I just get hungry and sleepy. This stuff, however, always works.'

'Does it make you feel happy?'

'More like euphoric. It lets me feel love towards the world and everyone in it. You want some?'

'I can't take pills. They get stuck in my throat.' Jane declined with a wave of his hand.

'What are you like when you're alone?' I slumped against the wall and took a drag from a cigarette.

'Why do you care?'

'Do you ever feel regret?'

Ignoring me, Jane began to choose a video cassette. 'Want to watch a Jean Harlow movie? Or maybe Theda Bara?'

He was smiling already.

'You're cruel.'

'You're right. Oh, what's this? It's called *My Love Has Disappeared*. I think the original English title is *Diary of a Mad Housewife*.'

'Since being with you, I can see just how pure I am. These days I'm *Juliet of the Spirits* all the way.'

'Oh, that's here too.'

'But it's the things I *don't* like about you that make me feel sorry for you. It makes me think about how hard it must be to live like you do. See, I begin by liking what I don't like about others. I'm a person of love.' I smiled faintly, like a masochist.

'Love is everything. Youth seems so wonderful! Life is beautiful,' Jane said in his superficial way. Then, he proceeded to do an exaggerated 'shaking with emotion and crying' act. I laughed lifelessly. When I asked him to 'pull a stupid face', he did it immediately. He let his eyes roll back and his mouth gaped lazily. He put on a funny voice.

'That was an idiot under a fig tree. Next up is an idiot wandering around a local high street.'

As always, I began to laugh. I felt a twinge of loneliness but I laughed anyway.

'If you don't want to watch a film, let's see if we can get some pirate radio on the go.' He fiddled with the tuner.

. . . is a request we received, but we don't have the record. So I'll sing it and play some random chords. Well then—Theeey asked me how I knewww . . .

'What's this supposed to be?'

' "Smoke Gets in Your Eyes," I think. I used to be a disc jockey,' he said.

. . . My true love was truuue . . .

'These days even the news is in DJ-speak. It's so irritating.'

'It's a frivolous culture.'

'But this is a good song. Do you know it? Apparently, Eva Braun used to sing it when she smoked because Hitler hated cigarettes.'

135

'Large-scale con-artists like him often have a spartan side to them. I also have an extremely stoic side to me. Don't laugh,' he said.

'Do you have some ambition you're not telling me about?'

'I do like to stand out. I'm thinking of going into entertainment. Something like that.'

'You can't be an actor,' I said frankly. 'A real actor needs to be able to feel things. Are you ever moved or inspired?'

'Of course not. When I'm being thankful, I think, "This is a moment when I should be thankful," and then I press start on my heart mechanism. Besides, I don't ever feel surprised.'

Suddenly, I felt the space that we occupied (a vague concept in itself) start to shrink and recede. Life as a fresh and complex entity was drying out and threatening to disappear fast. The caretaker of the soul hung his head low in shame.

'Oh dear, god has disappeared somewhere,' I screamed. Is this a bad trip from all the grim talk?

'God's down on the deep range,' Jane whispered quietly, almost like he was singing. Yes. God has left the monastery and may have met his end at the bottom of the sea.

'Is there a god for you?'

'There is.'

'Where?'

'I don't know.'

'Will he forgive you?'

'Nah.'

After a while, time began to flow more slowly.

I took a breath.

136

A wonderful moment – the joy of knowing that my own creation and the creation of the universe are intimately connected. The certainty that the present was predetermined. Yes, that's it. We will return millions of times over. Life might merely be a momentary bolt of lightning in the dark, after which the self melts into the infinite darkness. But it means that we will continue forever without interruption. I was filled with a baseless delight.

Time flowed even slower. It was taking on a sense of eternity.

Now! Now only happens now. But now exists everywhere. The past and future have vanished and countless nows continue infinitely. That is why I can keep going forever. I am completely free and can go to any now I choose. I can exist anywhere. Firmly, in any time.

'Are you hungry?' Jane purred.

I smoke two cigarettes once eleven o'clock rolls around. Thinking to myself that I really shouldn't do these things . . . I go to the bathroom anyway and swallow my pills. I take more each time.

My body is slightly feverish, always. I have no strength whatsoever. I feel so heavy that I can't do anything. Somewhere always hurts.

'Maybe I'll go see him tonight.' I'm talking to myself.

'Quit it with that guy,' the manager tells me sternly. 'There's nothing in it for you. Best case scenario is you getting knocked up with an unwanted baby. What is he to you anyway?'

The manager and Jane have become very hostile to each other.

'My paramour?' I pick up my bag. 'Yeah, I think I'll go see him.'

Time feels strange these days. I'm no longer able to change the speed of time according to my desires. Time has become patchy. It feels like it's passing by at a terrifying speed. Sometimes I have these momentary lapses of consciousness. It's like an episode of microsleep.

Before I know it, I'm outside Jane's apartment.

'You look tired,' he says, his eyes searching. 'What have you been up to since last week?'

Last week? It seems like only two or three hours ago that we last met. Oh, that's right. It was last week. But why does it feel so firmly attached to *now*?

'You've been acting strange, recently.' Jane anxiously wraps his arms around my neck.

'Maybe you're right.' I have no confidence. I feel like a puppet on a string. I'm being moved by someone else, with no will of my own.

'Are you taking the drugs?'

'Yes.'

'Why?'

'They give me relief. I'm probably headed towards destruction.'

Whose life is this? It's completely empty.

'Poor thing. Why do you hurt yourself so much? Is it on purpose?'

'Maybe so.' Not that it matters. Am I trying to make him a witness to my collapse? 'What kind of relationship are we in?' I whisper at him, moving my face closer.

'A stoic and static one.'

Is he struggling? Why does he struggle instead of me? Maybe I'm not actually struggling? Am I taking more drugs because he won't identify with me?

'I want to do something for you but I can't.' He nuzzles his fuzzy cheek against mine.

'You're probably the type who would feel regret if you killed someone. Even though you're cold.' I say something like that with my face and voice inexpressive. We never raise our voices.

'But I'm not cruel.'

'Yeah, that's right. The difference between cold and cruel is that to be cruel, you need to have feelings but to be cold, you don't, right?'

'Can you stop saying that?' Jane shakes his head. Is it so scary to watch another person self-destruct?

'I don't think I would feel any remorse about killing someone,' I continue. 'I don't know how I got this way. It's like I've crumbled into pieces. I'm starving for time. God has gone away somewhere. If someone invented a matter regeneration machine, it would be my god.'

He shakes his head.

I keep going. 'I have no remorse about having no remorse. So what can I do? I can only watch myself go to ruin.'

'Let's stop with this repressive relationship. It's not good. It's not good for you.' Jane's eyes look the same way they did when he watched me sleep. When was that? I can't remember.

'I'm driven only by my desires. Let me do what I like. God, I'm tired. I'm going to lie down.'

I get into bed and smoke.

I might have been in a daze. Quickly, it becomes light outside. Had morning come?

'I'm going mad.' I say to myself. When did time begin to flow so quickly? Next to me, Jane is asleep. I rack my brains and remember what we had done. We watched a film from the 1920s, we acted things out and laughed together. I remember the conversations and the facial expressions too. But I have no sense that it actually happened. Out of the blue, the thought comes to me: my skin is sagging.

While I spaced out, it became evening. Jane was gone. Around noon, I had eaten what he had made and listened to music, went for a walk then felt sick and came back. My memory is intact. Though it all feels like something that had happened to somebody else. No sensory recollections. It almost feels like an implanted memory. Also . . . he had left to meet someone for work.

It soon became late.

I started to get confused. It seemed I had begun to operate on a timeline entirely different from everybody else's. Jane comes home. He can't stand being around people for long so he comes back grumpy. Morning comes. I have to go to the bar. But there's no way that I can stand to work right now. I'll go back to my place. At night, I black out on the street. When I come to, I'm in my bed. Then night. Morning.

Time is related to memory. Maybe my ability to remember is getting weak. Is that why time keeps skipping? That means there's something wrong with my brain and . . . it's already Sunday. Oh, it's Sunday again.

There's something inside my empty brain, and that something expands at high speed. It's keeping memory from fastening on to anything. Every day feels like it's happening inside a dream.

Eventually, the concept of time started to disappear.

But that didn't mean that I was able to gain that feeling of eternity. I wasn't feeling that joy of the *now* being pressed down and eternally spread out.

The flow of time sped up. Or rather, for the most part, I wasn't fully aware of what I was doing. As a result, memory became more opaque and time was getting lost.

I knew vaguely that this might be a side effect of the drugs.

Jane came, and then people in white clothes came. I was taken somewhere far away. I was given an injection and questioned, and I responded in a trance. A green mark was put on my neck. A mark that I was mentally ill.

The artificial voice of the analysis computer was carefully crafted not to cause alarm. Questions were repeated over and over and over again. Injections and drugs, too. I was tied to the bed.

One morning, I came back.

The lump in my head was gone.

Time had returned.

It took two years and seven months. It felt like three days and it felt like thirty years. I looked in the mirror. And that's how I found out.

After getting back from the arcade, I didn't feel like going anywhere. I watched the 3-D television with the sound off.

My favourite thing is to be by myself. I can't take drugs, I don't smoke and I can barely drink, but I still know how to pass the time.

These days, I only work one day a week, if that. Right now, I do illustrations for a living, but I've had around twenty different jobs. Physical labour is better. I don't have to think about things. When I begin thinking, I start to dislike myself.

But, boy, today was terrible!

I really didn't want to remember Reiko. It was hard to see someone live that way. I didn't want to accept it . . . and in the end I couldn't accept it.

I stood up and turned off the TV. I'd one commission due the next week. I'll start it after I take a shower, I told myself.

There was a sound like someone flicking the door with their forefinger.

'Who is it?' I almost jumped. I don't even know why I'm so on edge. A memory associated with an old pain started to well up in me.

'Open up.'

I recognized the voice.

That old woman from the arcade was standing there.

'Uh, what's the matter? It's very late.' I scratched my head as casually as possible.

'I can't come by without a reason?'

Perhaps she followed me home? No way. The old lady pushed into my room. Her movements gave me a real shock. I'd seen them before, that dancer's grace. Was it really . . .?

A horrifying thought began to spread in me like a blot of ink, with a speed and intensity too powerful to resist.

'Oh, you've moved the bed.'

Reiko!

I didn't want to come to this realization. Even though I'd known, really, since I saw her at the arcade.

'Doing well?'

Reiko was trying to smile.

' . . . Yeah.'

I nodded. We often used to greet each other like this. When I was being introverted, I think she used to say, 'Cheer up,' or something like that.

'Oh, I'm so glad to hear it. You must have been surprised to see me.' Reiko twisted the sides of her lips oddly. Was she smiling beneath all those wrinkles?

'Yes. Very, or somewhat, anyway.'

I dislike situations like these. It was like a scene from a movie.

'It's thanks to you that I'm still alive.'

Was she being sarcastic?

'Not many good things came of it, though.'

I remained silent.

'You managed to protect yourself by acting worried but you didn't lift a finger for my sake, not really.'

She wasn't being accusatory. I knew that.

'You were scared that you were developing emotions. You couldn't help it. I get it, it scares everyone.'

Her appearance was truly pitiful. I couldn't believe the change.

'What have you been up to since then?'

I could feel my voice shaking. The back of my tongue was moistening. I knew what this meant. With my eyes open, tears began to fall.

'Stop it.' Reiko's voice was horribly kind. Like she was concerned for me. 'It's nothing to cry over.'

Reiko was trying to cheer me up, like she always would.

But this was too horrible. In only three years. When we first met, Reiko still had something of a wrecked beauty. Now, not even those ruins remained.

'I'm begging you . . .' Reiko said. She pulled a tissue out of a dirty, strangely shaped bag, and tried to wipe away my tears. Is this woman stupid? 'Come on, smile.'

Who smiles at a moment like this? But, after all, I'm the type who does whatever's asked. I placed a finger below each eye and forced my face to look like it was smiling.

'Play something for us,' Reiko said with her wrinkly face.

'What do you want?'

I couldn't get myself to look at her face properly. What am I even supposed to say? Do I say the same thing I used to? That I can't do anything for her?

'My eyes are bad these days. They won't stop watering. I just won't quit smoking, though, and the smoke gets in my eyes.'

So we played that old song. As the sound faded, Reiko looked at me.

'It can't be helped, eh?' Only her mouth was smiling. Her hair moved, and I saw on her neck a big discoloured scar. It looked like a powerful chemical had burnt it. In the hospital, they mark people. Had she tried to erase it herself? I couldn't say anything anymore.

Reiko narrowed her eyes and asked, 'I wonder if they've invented that matter regeneration machine yet.'

FORGOTTEN

Emma let out a squeal and froze in the darkness at the bottom of the stairs. The door to the first-floor bedroom was closed. Did this mean he was home? She had the feeling she'd left the door open when she went out earlier.

Her dissolute lifestyle lent itself to forgetting the little things.

In any case, Sol could well be in the bedroom. In which case, she had better hide her injection pendant. Emma reached out a hand to the wall and on came the light. She unfastened her bag and took out the pendant. There was still enough inside for a single hit.

Inside her bag, her fingers located a small perfume bottle. She rummaged around for some cotton pads and poured a little perfume onto one in lieu of surgical spirit. She rolled up her sleeve and wiped down her skin, then quickly applied the pendant.

A faint tingle of pain; she'd hit the same spot as before. But the sting soon vanished, and her skin grew hot. She could feel the liquid seeping in.

Good. Now she'd be able to sleep tonight.

Emma let out a long breath and began to climb the stairs. Her head was hot, and she felt herself becoming cheerier and a little reckless. Her fatigue eased and her body felt lighter.

'Aahh, who gives a shit, anyway?' But no sooner did this thought reach her lips than she found herself wondering, who gives a shit about what? Emma clung on to the banister, finally making it to the top of the stairs. She opened the door to find the room dark.

Her high was intensifying by the second. With eyes closed, she took off her clothes and hid her pendant under her pillow. She burrowed her way under the covers and then, feeling a sudden pang of thirst, turned on the light.

'Sol!'

He was standing there beside the bed.

'What are you doing?' Emma tried to say, but she was slurring badly. She must have taken too much.

'Thinking,' he said quietly.

'In the pitch dark?'

His green face loomed in closer. He was staring at her exposed skin, she realized. Hurriedly, she made to pull the sheet up to her chin. His hands stopped her, twisting her arm.

'Ow! That hurts!'

'Let me see.'

Emma shut her eyes. Sol's gaze affixed itself to the purple track marks on the inside of her arm. After a little while, he let go.

'Show me. Show me what you hid.' His voice was as quiet and measured as ever. She tried pinning him with a terrifying glare. His expression remained unchanged.

Emma pulled out the pendant from under the pillow. Sol took it from her and threw it down the rubbish chute.

'What did you do that for? What does it matter what I get up to, anyway? It's got nothing to do with you,' she objected futilely.

'That's hardly true. Keep this up and you'll be a junkie soon enough. Surely you can see that? If you wind up an invalid, I'm going back home.'

This reaction tickled Emma. So she was the reason Sol was staying here on Earth? But then she understood another layer of meaning to his words.

'You're saying if something bad happened to me, you'd just leave?'

Part of her sometimes wished that would actually happen. The burden of living with a Meelian was getting harder and harder to bear.

Emma's younger sister, who was married to the director of the Space Bureau, had told her that 'provincial sorts like that were to be pitied'. The planet Meele was underdeveloped, apparently. Emma's parents more or less agreed with this view, saying that Emma would be better off finding herself a nice Balian sergeant or a Kamiroyan musician, anything but a Meelian.

Emma herself thought that Sol was a bit too cerebral. Or maybe it was more that she was unable to give him what he wanted. She felt constricted. She'd come to believe, since being with Sol, that she was stupid. This wasn't a fun sensation. She hadn't yet cast off the kind of ambitions common to young people.

'I don't see what other choice I'd have. If you end up a junkie, you'll be a totally different person. Besides, I want to go back to Meele.'

'Oh, so that's what you call love, is it?' She pouted.

'I've never loved anybody, Emma.' He gave her a weak smile. Her pride was horribly wounded now.

'I've taken a fancy to a lot of girls, but that's different . . . That premonition I had when I met you, though – I don't think it was mistaken. I knew from the first you'd be the last woman I was with.'

Still staring at her, Sol began to remove his pyjamas. This was a quirk of his, wearing his pyjamas during the day while lounging about in the house. Sol turned his nose up at the dancing and music that Emma liked. So what did he do instead? Nothing. Three times a week, he would stop by the Alien Journalists' Club on the top floor of the Aerospace Bureau. The rest of the time he seemed to spend in his pyjamas, absorbed in thought.

Totally naked now, Sol got into bed.

'You know, I can never tell what's going on in that head of yours,' Emma said.

'That's because you're weak-minded,' he said, completely serious. He sounded irritated.

'Remind me again, what did you come to Earth to do in the first place?'

Was Sol actually a spy? It had been Emma's sister who'd first put that idea into her head. Initially she'd scoffed at it, but now she was becoming suspicious.

'I'm a poet.'

'Oh, don't give me that again!' Emma swerved from Sol's lips. Once they started kissing, she wouldn't be able grill him any further. Besides, she'd been in the arms of another man outside the apartment, and the taste and the feel of him still lingered with her.

'Don't make me repeat myself then.' Sol frowned at her.

'You couldn't even fill a school newsletter with the amount that you produce.'

'That's not a problem where I'm from. Our newspapers are less than half the size of the ones on Earth, and some days they're only four pages long. There's no evening paper, either. It's an easy-going sort of place. It's our agriculture and livestock that keep the place going. We've got a good climate. Nobody really wants an important job, and they only accept one out of a sense of duty. Even then, there's nothing pathological about the way that people work. Unlike your sister's husband, who only makes it home twice a week.'

'You've got mines on Meele too, though, right? Like the one where the big ruby you gave me came from. I lost that, by the way.'

'I'll get you another one when I go back. Hey, how about I take you back with me some time?' Sol stared at her intently as he said this.

Emma gave him a non-committal 'Hmm.'

In truth, she had no intention of doing any such thing at the moment. If the two of them went to Meele, Sol would probably end up working in a wind-turbine power station or something. She'd take care of the vegetable patch, enjoy the occasional afternoon stroll with him, have kids (yikes!)

and gradually get old. Once a year or so, he might give her a beautiful ring or bracelet, but she'd have no friends from Earth around to show them off to. The only Terrans around on Meele were the piratical mine-raiders, hiding behind their Scientific Investigation Commission accreditation, and tourists who were hot on far-flung destinations. Terrans didn't have the best reputation over there, thanks to their tendency to dig everything and anything up.

Sol took his cigarettes from the shelf on the headboard.

'How will you cope, though, if you ever do go back to Meele? You say the Terran air has tainted me, but that's gotta be true of you too, after all these years.'

Sol brought the cigarette to his lips, blew out a plume of smoke, and answered.

'I'll give up smoking if I go back. I've been here fifteen years, though – it's only natural that I've picked up some of the Terran vices.'

Sol's parents had come to Earth as goodwill ambassadors. But when their term of service ended, they had both become mentally ill and returned home. Sol, whose Terran education had been publicly funded, had spent most of his adolescence here – if you defined adolescence as between the ages of fifteen and twenty.

A year on Sol's home planet was just four days longer than on Earth. Sol would soon be turning thirty.

'I'm not talking about smoking! I mean, you get irritated quickly. Most Meelians are good-natured and contemplative, and quiet to boot. It's not the quietude of pure saints, though – they're quiet like the best boxers are quiet.'

150

Hitting upon this expression, which seemed to her to have a nice, philosophical ring to it, Emma felt a tinge of satisfaction. It was in fact an expression she'd heard Sol himself use, about a month previously – though she didn't remember this.

Sol cast his eyes down, displaying his deep-green eyelashes. The hair falling across his forehead was the same shade of green.

'So you're saying I'm different from other Meelians?'

His eyelashes lifted, and a pair of violet eyes peered out at Emma. Sol stubbed out his cigarette.

'Don't you think you've developed quite a temper, compared to how you used to be? My sister's friend went to the same university as you. She was telling me how you used to be back then.'

Sol had entered university at the age of fifteen.

He adjusted his pillow and lay looking up at the ceiling. As she took in his profile, Emma thought back to the man she'd been with earlier on. She figured he'd wanted to sleep with her, but then he didn't try and get her back to his room or make any heavy moves, not really, so now she wasn't so sure. He'd approached her in the ice-cream parlour, asking her about Meelian sexuality.

'They're dirty as you like. Psychologically speaking, I mean,' Emma had told him.

'Do they do it like Terrans?'

'It's not like I've slept with hundreds of Terrans, and the only Meelian I know about first-hand is Sol. I couldn't possibly know.'

The man had wanted specifics. Emma evaded his questions, giving playful answers. If he'd only responded with a little cunning and persistence, she thought wistfully, they could have had a lot of fun. As far as Emma was concerned, these sorts of amorous games were the among the best of life's offerings. And, yet, it was only in the first three months or so of her relationship with Sol that he'd seemed properly into her, and that she'd felt truly happy. When it came to satisfying her sense of pride, Emma was more covetous than an old loan shark. (Come to think of it, Emma's grandma was a loan shark!)

'Maybe it's the air here that does it. That chemical found in tiny quantities in the Terran atmosphere. That's why you lot forget everything.' Sol was mumbling as if speaking to himself.

'I don't forget things!' Emma tweaked the flesh of his cheek and he turned to face her.

'Not while they're still going on, no. But as soon as something's over, it's as if it never happened. Same with war, even. I went back and looked through the records from 1950 onwards. What with us living in Tokyo and your parents' commitment to their Japanese heritage, I decided to see how much people remember of the Korean and Vietnam wars. I looked into the records from the American side too.'

'But we're not in the age of Japan and America anymore! Now we've got a World President. I know a lot of people say it's just for show, but still. Even the capital city moves periodically!'

'Sure, on the surface it's as you say. But in reality, people are more concerned with what country they're from than the fact they're Terrans. In the USA, people used to worry about whether they were of Italian or Irish heritage or whatever. Then there were several generations when people of all different heritages began to mix together, and now we're seeing the emergence of an American race, although it's still only in its formative stages. Which means that everyone's only serving their own national interests, just like they used to in the past. Don't you think that's odd? In an age where there are so many spaceships being built and everyone supposedly has their eyes trained on what lies beyond their own planet, each and every nation is looking to become something like the British Empire. They all want theirs to be the empire where the sun never sets on the seven seas or whatever . . . I don't remember the exact wording they used, but that's the rough meaning. Now they're looking for planets to colonize, just as in the past they used to claim other nations. Lots of Terrans have been showing up on Meele, too. The Meelians have had enough of it and have begun to restrict the influx.'

Both of them could get really passionate when they got talking, especially Sol.

'It's messed up. But doesn't that contradict what you were saying before?'

'In what way?' he asked her, his eyes now tinged with blue.

'What you were saying about Terrans being forgetful. The concept of nationhood didn't disappear with the founding of the World Federation. Doesn't that prove that people haven't forgotten their love for their own country?'

'Oh, Emma, what a naïve little girl you are. Can't you see it's got nothing whatsoever to do with love for one's country? If anything, it's a form of territorial egotism. People don't like having a rubbish dump outside their front door, that's all it comes down to. Isn't the Tokyo Garbage War still going on to this day?'

Sol smiled wryly. The second part of what he'd said made zero sense to Emma.

'But there aren't any rubbish dumps any more, Sol! Even my mother and father have never seen one,' she snapped back at him.

'It's a metaphor. Sheesh, talking with you is exhausting! I have to explain every last thing!'

'I guess it's like that with all of us stupid Terrans, eh?'

'Hey, don't get mad. You're right, though, for the most part. Though it's different with the telepathic ones. Then the conversation goes a bit smoother. Although in truth, the telepathic skills of the Terrans I've met are nothing to write home about, and they can't read all your thoughts. Thank goodness – that'd be awful, no? If someone could see absolutely everything you were thinking?'

What are you saying, Sol? Are you trying to tell me you've got something to hide? Something you don't want anyone to find out? That you are carrying out some kind of plot here on Earth, after all? But then as Emma was thinking this, a different suspicion crossed her mind. When she started down the path of doubt, there was no end to it.

'So are you telepathic then?' she asked with as much affected casualness as she could muster.

'Nope,' said Sol, plain as you like.

'Not even a little bit?' Emma looked at him probingly. He smiled, reached out a hand and mussed her hair.

'My powers of understanding are greater than yours. That must be what made you think that. It seems to me that Meelians are better at understanding one another than Terrans. It's the

Mirinnians who have the greatest telepathic powers, although their comprehension of language and thought patterns is pretty low. Even if they can read the minds of people from other planets, there's not that much they can do with that information.'

Sol's hand drifted down from Emma's hair to her cheek. As his eyes rested on her, they assumed that soft, slightly hazy look which she liked best of all. Just as she sensed he would, he leaned in and kissed her.

What did he mean that Terrans were quick to forget? What was he referring to in particular? Sol always found a way of glossing over everything. Now, when she thought about it, she realized that with his clever linguistic flourishes he'd managed to pull the wool over her eyes hundreds of times. She was finding it harder and harder to put the parts of Sol together and make sense of him as a whole. Was that because he expressed himself in such a complex way? And yet she was pretty sure that, at heart, he was a pretty straightforward guy.

But as he began to slip the straps of her vintage-style slip from her shoulders, Emma felt her concern for such matters evaporate.

'Have you only ever slept with Terran women?'

Sol lifted his head from where it was buried in her chest. At first, he would roll his eyes and smile in exasperation when she probed him with questions like this, but not anymore.

'No. I mean, intercourse with Mirinnians isn't physically possible because they're built so differently, but Balinians, Kamiroyans and Terrans are all sexually compatible with Meelians. Although it's only Meelians and Terrans who can produce offspring, so maybe we're actually the most compatible of the interplanetary pairings. I'd need to look into it . . . Anyway, I mean, I'm not particularly eclectic in my tastes, and I'm not interested in anything that feels too much like hard work. The Kamiroi aesthetic doesn't really do it for me, although I hear that you Terrans really go for it. And Balians are way too irrational.'

'So how are Terrans different from Meelian girls?'

This time, Sol didn't raise his head to answer. 'They're built differently. The girls where I'm from have pretty great figures. There was this one girl I was with who was just beautiful, crazy sexy, with this amazing body—'

'What are you doing with me, then? If I'm that unattractive in comparison.' Emma's breathing was ragged and heavy. Sol looked up at her.

'Look, we're together, aren't we? So what does it matter? In all these fifteen years, I've only ever lived with one other girl. For three years, I lived with my parents. After they went back, I had to live in an apartment so small you'd have barely believed it, cooking for myself on an old-style gas burner.' There were flames blazing at the back of Sol's eyes.

'Couldn't you have stayed in the student dorms?'

'To borrow your bigoted Terran terminology, Meele is a *backward* planet. I had no choice but to stand there and look on dumbly as the folks from all the other planets skilfully outmanoeuvred me to get the good rooms. That was how it was back then. And now, look! Suddenly your government decides to put me up in an amazing place like this, and for free. Earth is getting smaller, but here I am living in an apartment with two bedrooms, a living room, and a home bar in the kitchen.

I'm not even the official Meele correspondent – that's some other guy. I'm writing mostly for the magazines, rather than the newspapers. And, yet, all of a sudden, they land me with this room – doesn't that seem a bit fishy to you?' Sol's face was tense.

'I guess,' said Emma, non-committally.

'What's more, so that people wouldn't get suspicious, your government requested similar kinds of apartments for all the correspondents they sent to Meele, of whom there are many. There's an obvious intention behind that move. By sending in people in such large numbers, they're trying to advertise the fact that Terrans have an interest in Meele. Well, frankly speaking, that "interest" is more trouble than it's worth. Interest signifies future invasive action, if Terran history is any guide. I forget when it was now, but there was this guy who came to Earth on the run from Meele. As far as the Meelians were concerned, he was a criminal. His spiritual powers had sunk to the level of a crooked Terran businessman. Anyway, after carrying out a thorough assessment of his psychological state, the Terran government used him in formulating a sort of profile of what Meelians are like. I'm sure that was the basis on which they concluded they could travel over to Meele in safety, and that if it ever came to military conflict, they'd have the upper hand.' Sol shut his mouth and retreated back inside his own head, as he always did.

'You want a drink?' Emma broke into his silence, as she always did.

'Hmm? Ah, yeah, okay.'

'Go get one, then.'

'I can't be bothered to put my clothes back on.' He reached his hands behind his head.

'Pfft, same goes for me! I always knew your planet was old-fashioned and conservative. Getting the women to do everything for you!'

The planet of Meele had plentiful natural resources. One working person could easily provide enough for an entire household. In their youth, Meelian women would spend three or four years out in society (how old-fashioned it sounded to even say that!), before deciding on an appropriate partner and settling down as housewives.

'That's not true, I'm just exhausted today. Go on, please. I'll listen to whatever you say afterwards.' He made the sweet face he pulled whenever he was trying to win her round.

'Pfft.' Emma got out of bed and began to get dressed. With great care, she wrapped her shawl around her shoulders.

'Ah, what a beauty! I chose the right woman to give my pure heart to.'

'What rubbish you come out with! We all know how pure that heart of yours is. I might as well keep it by the door and use it as a shoe rag.'

Emma opened the door and went downstairs. She left the bedroom door open for when she came up carrying the glasses.

'The reincarnation of Brigitte Bardot. The third coming of Claudia Cardinale. Monica Vitti's younger cousin. Or else, Juliet of the Spirits. Gloria Wandrous from *BUtterfield 8*.' Even at the bottom of the stairs, she could hear the old-movie buff droning on and on.

'No, that's not it! She's Bud Powell's *Cleopatra's Dream*. She's Bokko-chan.'

What was he talking about, honestly? Emma went to the bar, first mixing a drink for herself: a screwdriver. That disappeared soon enough, so she made another. She felt like getting obliterated. Tonight was not the night for playing innocent with a gin fizz or some other sickly-sweet cocktail.

What on Earth was Sol thinking? Were all Meelian men like him? 'Territorial egotism'? When he put it like that, of course it sounded objectionable, but the truth was intelligent creatures tended to have a healthy dose of egotism – quite aside from whatever needs they might have. Yet, immediately, Sol's retort to this floated up in Emma's mind: 'But Terrans are extremely mentally unstable. Their stubborn egotism isn't complete. My home planet is no match for Earth in terms of scientific and technological development, but at least most people there consider how they want to live their lives. Our history is unfathomably long, and yet there have been only five wars recorded – including a couple of really small-scale ones. And the last of those wrapped up over two millennia ago.'

Emma's second drink had disappeared as swiftly as the first. They were out of orange juice. She diluted some vodka with water and clambered up onto the barstool.

War – would there really be an interplanetary war? No, surely not. Earth had been getting along well (superficially, at least) with all the other planets. Over thirty years had elapsed since Earth had discovered Meele.

Emma's head was spinning, like the time she'd contracted acute pneumonia. It must have been alcohol mingling with the last hit she'd taken. She attempted to grab hold of the bar, but it was too late. She slid right off the stool and struck the side of her head, hard, against the counter on her way down

Her body had turned to jelly. She felt powerful arms peel her from the floor.

'I thought you were taking a while, so I came downstairs to see what was going on, only to find you like this. Oof, you're heavy! What's going on, Emma? You've been acting strange of late.' Sol picked her up.

'Ah, my shawl.'

'Leave that for now. You can get it later.' He began to carry her upstairs.

'But it's my favourite!'

Sol didn't answer. Stepping carefully under her weight, he ascended the stairs.

Oh Sol, when you hold me like this I'm done for. By now I've come to admit (albeit reluctantly) that I do love you. I can't stand that that's true. I've fallen for several men in the past, but you're the first person I've ever felt serious about. The very idea that I would fall in love with a man, that class of people I secretly feel such contempt for . . . I hate you for making it happen.

'Did you say something?' Sol asked, as they entered the bedroom.

'No.' Emma shook her head. She could feel herself lapsing into misery. He tucked her into bed.

'One day, Sol, you and I . . .'

There would come a time when they would accept one another entirely. One day that time would come – it had to come.

'When I'm a senile old lady.'

Sol laughed a little, then retreated into himself. In Meelians, night-time was characterized by a combination of psychological disengagement and sleep. When Sol spoke of his dreams, did he not in fact mean his waking fantasies?

Emma gave up thinking and closed her eyes. In the morning, she decided, she would go and see her friend who was studying pharmacology; she would get herself another pendant and a new supply of drugs. There was no way anyone could live in a world like this with a fully functioning mind. You only found yourself feeling angry from morning until night. If she ended up joining some kind of political movement as a result, her mother and father would be upset. Using drugs, she told herself, was her way of being a good daughter.

Sol turned over and wrapped his arms around her. She lay there, her eyes open, as the night wore on.

'You shouldn't do too much of this,' Luana said as she handed Emma a small baggie. It was afternoon, and the two of them were sitting on the café terrace eating some odd-looking fruit imported from Meele.

'Yeah, I know. Thanks.'

Emma put the baggie away inside a large bag made of fabric woven from tree bark. Earth relied on Meele for almost half of its agricultural produce, such as this bark; it been woven by Kamiroyans in a Martian factory.

'I don't think you understand. It's fine by me if you get addicted. What I mean is, whatever way you look at it, this stuff has a devastating effect on your personality.'

Luana placed both her elbows on the table and leaned in towards Emma.

'Keep it up for long and you'll find your willpower weakening. You'll be easily swayed by external suggestions and instructions. In that sense, it's similar to Scopolamine. It makes you forget the passions and principles you once had.' Luana had a deathly serious look to her.

'Does it make you lose your memory?' Emma narrowed her eyes. What Sol had said about forgetting had stuck with her.

'No, it's more like the vividness of your emotions fades. You start to feel like the you from the past was mistaken about all kinds of things. The past you becomes unrecognisable. Who benefits from that, I wonder?'

'But the state is cracking down on it,' Emma said, lowering her voice.

'That's only for show, though. I mean, it's still popular, isn't it? You know they've recently announced a drug that makes people less susceptible to fear.' Luana was frowning, as she was prone to do.

'Why, though?' Emma asked stupidly.

The Mirinnian waiter approached, and the two fell silent. The waiter began to clear the table with two of his tentacles, keeping the other two hanging neatly by his sides.

'Would you like anything else?' he asked, although he already knew the answer.

'No, we're done.' Luana stood up.

'Mirinnians gross me out,' Emma murmured once they'd paid and got out onto the street.

'What about them? Their bodies?'

The pair began heading down towards the entrance to the Subterrail.

'No, more like that you have absolutely no idea what they're thinking. They're so expressionless.'

'Maybe they're not thinking about anything. You know, a professor from ____ University tried to develop their telepathic abilities. But they were no help to him whatsoever. Apparently they could only pick up simple words.'

The platform was deserted. Emma leaned up against the wall and thought about where she should go next.

'Where's Sol?' Luana pulled out a cigarette designed to help you quit smoking from her bag and put it to her lips.

'I don't know,' Emma replied honestly.

'My boyfriend will have cleaned the room, done three days' worth of washing and will right about now be roasting us a chicken.' Luana smiled with evident satisfaction. Emma pouted.

'Don't you think Sol might be with another woman? He's quite a catch, after all.' Luana contorted her lips as she asked this, suppressing a smile.

Emma had never even considered such a possibility. She'd been too caught up in her thoughts of herself. But come to think of it, Sol did sometimes stay out overnight.

'Where can you get those tiny spy cameras? Would they let someone like me buy one?' Just voicing the question made Emma blush.

'For surveillance? You can buy them anywhere, and you don't need a licence or anything. The buttonhole type is the most common. Although if the wearer undresses, all you'll see is the ceiling.'

The shuttle compartment drew up to the platform.

'Go ahead,' Emma said. She'd given up on her plans to return home.

'Okay then. Don't get too het up about this though, okay?' Luana opened the door and stepped inside, and Emma watched her press the button and speak her desired destination into the microphone. Emma waved. Once the compartment had disappeared, she took the escalator leading up to ground level.

Emma was looking at a small screen, which showed the face of a Meelian man.

'That's not true. People from our planet aren't that immature,' the man was saying. The voice, filtered as it was through the automatic translation device, was high and shaky. Naturally, the two men were talking in their native tongue.

'You're quite the optimist, aren't you! How do you know there's not going to be another Opium War?' Sol's low voice sounded close to the microphone.

'Oh, I forgot you'd studied Terran history. Which country was it again that smuggled opium to China then tried to colonize it? But in any case, isn't our conception of pleasure slightly different from those on Earth? It's sex and drugs that does it for them. Or else, speed, thrills, suspense. In other words, that giddy feeling.' There was a faint smile on Jebba's face as he spoke.

'That's true. Whereas we can always disengage. That's not pleasure, exactly – it's something deeper,' Sol said seriously.

'So how are the Terran women?' Jebba asked, teasingly. Emma readjusted her posture.

'They're good.' Sol said, straight-faced.

'What's good about them?'

Sol must have moved, for now the camera showed only half of Jebba's face. Where the other half had been, Emma could now see a curtained window. It was a shabby apartment somewhere.

'Their race knows sadness, but it doesn't come to the forefront of their consciousness. We know sadness too. In fact, if anything our sense of sadness is better defined. But between the two of our races, it's the Terrans who are the more tragic. They have limits in the form of decrepitude and death.'

'Do you feel proud that death is something you have to choose?'

'Yes.'

'Even if that choice is occasioned through despair?'

'Despair is an incredibly deep, clear emotion. In a way, it's similar to the very peak of psychic disengagement. That's why it's not really accompanied by sadness.'

'Your parents went half a year ago, right?'

Emma's ears pricked up at Jebba's words. What did he mean by 'went'?

'If I was a Terran, I'd have wailed and wept when it happened. Scholars from Earth are up in arms about the suicide rate on our planet. They don't understand why we do it, when we could live for longer. Even some Meelians don't understand despair. Then you end up like that person who lived for six hundred years.'

'Did you hear they died recently? In an accident – a totally meaningless death. To think of someone living that long and never understanding despair.'

'That's what was so impressive about my parents' death. Of course what they did was nothing unusual, but when it's your own parents, it feels different. From about half a day before they went, I felt their consciousness moving inside me. Wherever Meelians are when they die, their family members always know. I didn't fully understand what was going on, but it moved me.' Sol's voice grew rich with emotion.

'I can imagine.' Jebba's eyes had taken on a tender hue.

'But Terrans aren't entirely a lost cause. In some cases, the limitation placed on their lives gives them a powerful energy. That's especially true of women. Their field of interest is terribly narrow. They're primitive and strong. If we could somehow—'

'Use that?' offered Jebba.

'I don't like putting it that way. And, no, that's not what I mean,' Sol said, apparently struggling.

'Okay, then. You mean —?'

Jebba cut out for an instant. The red cannot-translate light flickered on. It must have been a word unique to the Meelian language, Emma thought.

'Yes.' It seemed as though Sol nodded. Emma, who was growing uneasier by the second, made to turn off the switch. Use that? She felt enraged that Sol shared only such a tiny fraction of himself with her. His affection for her was all a pretence – a sham, a poor imitation. What an idiot I've been, she thought.

'I've had an idea. I'm going to head off,' Sol stood up.

'Bye, then,' Jebba said.

Sol would likely be back soon, Emma thought, and touched a finger to the screen. The automatic translation device went

166

black, so that at a glance, it looked like just a regular compact mirror. She shut it away in her dresser drawer and went downstairs.

Two weeks had passed since that eye-opening conversation with Luana. After thinking it over a long while, Emma had taken the decision to switch a button on Sol's jacket for a concealed camera.

Emma moved to the front of the bar and took down a bottle of Mirinnian spirits from the shelf. The pearl-coloured liquid swirled around inside the bottle. It had been a present from her older sister. Emma took off the lid and a bittersweet medicinal aroma permeated the air.

The glasses were dirty. She opened the lid of the dishwasher and put a glass inside. In twenty seconds, the indicator light went out. She removed the glass and poured herself some of the liquor.

What was she supposed to do? The tension she'd felt while staring at the screen evaporated and she was left with a feeling of utter exhaustion. Honestly, she felt like a dog that had just collapsed and died.

Emma drank. The drink had no taste, only a cold, smooth texture. And all this when I've given up drugs and have been being so well behaved, she thought. Soon she'd be out of money. She'd have to go and ask her father for some. Emma had been out of work for a year and a half now, since she'd quit her job at the Space Bureau after falling out with her boss.

The Space Bureau – yes, if Sol had some motive for being with her, it may well have something to do with her job there.

Quite possibly, he'd been trying to trick her into stealing classified documents for him. But then she'd gone and quit . . .

But, no, that couldn't be true. She'd just been a low-level employee, loading tapes into computers. She highly doubted they'd store any top-secret information on the computers. Things only made it there once their plans had taken a certain degree of shape. If Sol had wanted someone dealing with things that never made it to surface level, he'd have targeted the director's secretary.

Emma pictured the secretary. She'd got divorced a long while back and seemed to have been single ever since. She was into her forties now, but was still pretty attractive . . .

Emma topped up her glass.

What was she doing, anyway, pursuing such a ridiculous train of thought? Trying to establish a link between Sol and the secretary – honestly! And yet, she was convinced Sol was trying to ensure the protection of his home planet. How could such a thing be achieved? If it came down to sheer military force, Meele wouldn't last a second. And Earth would hardly go starting a war without a reason.

A reason: they could accuse the Meelians of plotting against Earth – it didn't even matter if it was a total fabrication – and then spread the idea. The Meelians carry some kind of terrible germ, something like that would do. No, on second thoughts, that was no good. They carried out stringent scans and disinfection at the spaceport. If anything, Terrans were the ones spreading disease. Just recently, there'd been an outbreak of a Terran strain of influenza on Meele. Earth-dwelling Meelians would occasionally die of a brief cold. For them, dying before they'd fulfilled their potential, before they'd attained either absolute despair or the resolve to die, must have been truly tragic.

Emma propped an elbow on the counter. The alcohol was gradually going to her head. Her body felt floppy and hot. Those deceitful Meelian motherfuckers!

Outside, the day grew dimmer.

Sol still wasn't back. What was taking him so long?

She reached a hand inside her pocket. There were two notes and a few coins in there. She could roughly calculate how much she had without looking. What a miserly little skill she'd managed to acquire for herself!

Emma picked up her coat and left the house, heading for the restaurant on the corner. There was a Meelian waiter working there – could she not avoid them? With a glum face, Emma made her way through soup, bread and an omelette. She was making to leave, without indulging in an after-dinner coffee, when a man walking in greeted her. 'Hi!'

Who was this again?

'Do you live around here? I've forgotten.'

Ah, yes, this was the guy who'd escorted her home recently. His name was . . . Ceno.

'Are you alone?'

'Yes,' Emma answered, looking at the ground.

'You don't seem too happy, what's up? Will you have a coffee with me?'

Taking the decision for her, Ceno took a seat by the window, raising a hand to order two coffees.

'I'd like mine weak.'

The place only played old music: there was 'Time of the Season' and 'Sunny', followed by 'Also Sprach Zarathustra'. Now they were playing Raymond Lafèvre's 'La Reine de Saba'.

'I live round here too. Why don't you come up to my place?' Ceno said with the utmost casualness when they were midway through their coffees.

'Hmm . . .' Emma was in the mood for a bit of fun, but there was something about Ceno that felt hard to pin down. He said he was working for a TV station, but it was impossible to say if that was true. Now Emma remembered a guy she'd dated a while back who, when they'd fought, had come out with the most awful insults in a supposedly ironic way (like a glimpse behind the scenes at Hollywood). About the least offensive of his offerings was 'you filthy mucous membrane'. Why had she suddenly thought of him?

'Not today.'

'Really? Why so cold, eh?'

Emma hated being spoken to like this. She held her breath, then exhaled slowly.

'Did I say something wrong?' Ceno's words expressed concern, but he looked annoyed. Have I started viewing men differently since being with Sol? she wondered. Oh, Sol, you swindling swine!

'I'm going home.' Emma stood up.

'I'll walk you.' Ceno also got to his feet, taking advantage of the moment to squeeze her hand, ever so naturally. She pulled it away, fearfully.

Back home, Emma made a beeline for the bar, not climbing the stairs. She was getting very fond of that pearl-coloured drink.

A noise from above. Emma flinched, almost dropping her glass. Sol must be back.

Then Emma heard something that could have been a mirror breaking. Had he worked out that it wasn't just a regular compact?

'Emma!' Hearing a harsh voice from upstairs, Emma hugged the bottle close. 'Come upstairs.'

Casting a look up the stairs, Emma saw Sol's face in the doorway, oddly pale, his expression twitchy.

'I don't want to.'

'Just come up.'

Reluctantly, Emma forced a smile. 'You promise not to get angry?'

For a brief moment, Sol gave her the very faintest of smiles. 'I promise. Just come up.'

With the bottle and two glasses in hand, Emma slowly made her way upstairs.

'What's this?' Sol pointed to the bits of the screen now strewn across the floor.

'It's a mirror.'

Sol's eyes glinted with a fierce light. He stared down at the ruined screen for a while.

'Yes, I can see it's a mirror.' He seated himself on the bed. 'A mirror with an inbuilt translation device,' he added, as if speaking to himself. How did he know?

'Would you, um . . . like a drink?'

'Are you an alcoholic now?' Sol's voice was calm and restrained. He didn't take his eyes off Emma.

'No.'

'Yeah, I'll have a drink.'

She handed him a glass and poured him some of the liquor. Sol wasn't wearing a jacket. She looked round and saw it on the chair. Its third button had been ripped off.

'Luana found it. She's a sharp one.'

Luana? But she was the one who'd egged Emma on! Surely not her, that didn't make sense. Had she deliberately tried to incite Emma's jealousy?

'When did you two meet?' Emma tried to sound casual, but her voice was trembling.

'You introduced us, half a year or so ago.'

'I didn't!' Anger flared up in Emma.

'But we only got friendly about ten days ago. There's something I needed her help with.'

'So you used her. Like you did me.'

'Tell me when exactly I used you.' Sol's tone was forceful.

'Don't get angry. You're the one who said it.'

'So you were watching? Well, in that case you'll know that it wasn't me that said it. It was Jebba.'

'Yes.'

Emma's tears took her by surprise. Once she'd begun to cry, there was no chance of her stopping. She stood stock still, clutching her glass as the tears rolled down her face.

'What a rotten man you are!' Her voice was trembling – trembling so much it was hard to get the words out.

'That's not true. You've misunderstood.' Sol stood up and went to embrace her. 'I was trying to get Luana to get us stuff – reagents, drug samples and so on. That's why I needed to get friendly with her.'

'Don't touch me. You can't fool me like that.' Sol ran his fingers through her hair.

'She has her suspicions about the Space Bureau's methods, you see. They look for other planets' weak spots and then try to worm their way into the holes. For them Meele is just a . . . come on, stop crying! What's wrong?' Sol attempted to raise her chin. Emma resisted.

'I'm not crying any more . . . But you're a spy, aren't you?'

He snorted. 'Your way of thinking is so childish! A spy? It's your friend that's the spy.'

In the soft light of the room, Sol's face had resumed its regular expression. The tense paleness had gone.

'Who?'

'The man who brought you to the door. Where did you meet him?'

'Does that matter? He's just some guy I know. Not a friend, and definitely not the kind of friend that—'

'I'm not questioning the nature of your relationship,' Sol cut her off sharply. 'I'm asking where you met him.'

'Um . . . Outside the hat shop. I was standing by the window.'

'Oh. Who started the conversation?'

'He approached me, obviously!'

'Really?' He peered into her eyes.

'Really.'

Sol sat down on the bed. With his slippered toes, he attempted to draw the broken screen close to him.

'This breaks just like a mirror. Designed so that people suspect nothing . . . What's his name?' Sol shook his head, moving the hair that had fallen across his forehead.

173

'Ceno.'

'And what does he do?'

'He said he works in TV.'

Sol said nothing for a while. Emma poured liquor into their glasses and sat down beside him.

'Would it bother you if war broke out between Earth and Meele?' he asked finally, in an extremely kind and gentle voice – the kind of voice people used with children or the simple-minded.

Emma felt like she might cry again. 'Yes.'

She felt like she was standing alone, barefoot and totally exhausted, in the depths of the night.

'Why?'

'Because you'd be put in a camp or something.'

'You wouldn't want to leave me?'

'I don't think so,' Emma replied, without confidence.

'You don't think so. That's so typically you.' Sol grinned.

'Is there going to be a war?'

'Lately I've been feeling like one's coming. Yesterday, when I got off the Subterrail, I came over all dizzy and then my mind filled with all kinds of images.'

'What'll happen to us?' Emma asked in a frail voice. Sol hung his arms between his knees and lowered his head. In a very low voice he said, 'I had a vision of you dying.'

'Struck by a bomb?'

'No. You were on a bed. It doesn't mean it's going to happen soon. Maybe in a few years . . . I mean, in a few decades everyone alive on Earth now will be dead anyway.'

'True,' Emma said, but inside she felt wretched. The majority of Meelians took their own lives. It was death, just the same

174

as what befell the Terrans, and yet it was totally different. Sol was an alien.

Emma squeezed his hand.

'There's nothing to be frightened of,' he said.

'Right.' Emma's head also began to droop.

'How do you feel about the idea of getting out of here?'

Emma knew what Sol was thinking, so she replied quietly, 'Not as badly as I used to. But I don't completely trust you.'

'You're so honest.' He patted her head. 'Honest and good.'

'Although I do feel like I'm coming to trust you.'

'You see? Did you watch me with Luana?'

Emma shook her head.

'You didn't? Well that's a relief.' Sol gave a cheery smile. It was as if he was trying to cheer her up.

'Was it full-on?' Emma smiled for the first time that day.

'Yes, pretty full-on.'

'Enough to make me lose trust in you?'

'Yes, most likely.'

A faint bitterness spread through her. Was this jealousy? But, no, as far as Luana was concerned, it wasn't jealousy that Emma felt. This was a feeling she'd had before. Without being aware of it, Emma was jealous of Sol's very existence in this world.

Sol was impossible to understand.

Even when she clung to him like this, she felt that the largest part of him was off wandering through some unknown territory all alone. Even in her arms, he was always able to liberate himself from her, to make himself free. She envied him that. Sol was an alien.

'What is it?'

'I feel so lonely.'

'That feeling will go away when you learn to trust me completely.'

'Complete trust is a delusion.' Emma rested her head on his shoulder.

'What about complete forgiveness, then?'

'Complete forgiveness . . .' Emma lifted her head and looked at him. Then she said very slowly, 'That's really difficult. I don't think I can do it.'

'But if you could, you wouldn't feel lonely.'

'True,' she agreed weakly.

'The thing about you is that you're never satisfied.' Emma knew that he wasn't talking about any rational satisfaction – he was talking about her spiritual condition. Now he wrapped her in his arms.

'Ceno is a fake name. Jebba did some research on him when he was making a list of all the people connected with the Information Bureau. I got a real surprise when I looked out the window and saw him standing there, I tell you.'

The world around them went on moving, regardless of their desires or their feelings, like a huge river. Its surface might appear calm, but charging along its bottom was a fast, powerful current, exerting a silent pressure on them.

Emma was enveloped in a feeling of unbearable loneliness.

'Take off your clothes,' Sol instructed. Emma took off her jumper, then pulled down her tight-fitting slitted skirt. The type of clothing she wore was no longer in fashion. Nowadays, men and women alike wore boiler suits made of coarse fabric.

On top they would wear metallic coats or chunky knitted mantles. Sol had once said the way she dressed was 'wonderfully kinky', but that 'it would land even better with more of a 1930s twist'. He always expressed himself bluntly and honestly, which gave him an air of incredible innocence.

'If only your stockings had seams. Have you heard of garters? Those wide elastic bands people used to wear to hold their stockings in place?' Sol said, as he watched Emma taking off her clothes.

'Yeah, I saw a picture of some in a book about fashion history. You see them in old films sometimes too.'

'Black garters embroidered with red roses – ah, they drive me wild.'

'Where did you hear about them?'

'Oh, the same place as you,' Sol said, caught off guard and seeming to panic slightly.

'They're expensive though, and really hard to track down. Get me some next time.'

'Mmm,' Sol hummed non-committally. From out of her melancholy, Emma gazed at the green face that came looming over her.

Emma hadn't slept the previous night – Sol hadn't come back to the apartment. Two months had passed since the smashed-screen incident, and the atmosphere between them had grown increasingly intolerable.

Thanks to her insomnia, she'd come over all sleepy in the afternoon. She eventually got into bed at six in the evening. She'd not been asleep twenty minutes when Sol woke her.

'We've got to go. Leave everything behind.'

She understood what he meant.

Into a large bag, Emma stuffed a couple of books and some sleeping pills. Cinebooks would probably have been a better option than old-style paper – they were less bulky, which meant she could have taken more. But cinebooks required special contact lenses to read – if you ran out, you were done for. Emma had to remind herself: she didn't know where she was going.

In the entranceway, she moved to step into her red high heels, but Sol stopped her. She pouted and went instead for some flats, although it seemed to her a terrible shame.

Sol didn't utter a word during the heli-taxi trip. That fact alone conveyed the urgency of the situation.

When they arrived at Jebba's apartment, he was waiting for them outside. There were two others there too, both Meelians.

'We're going to dye your hair and skin green. Don't worry, it's just stage foundation so you can easily remove it with this spray. It won't come off if you sweat either,' the woman explained in an accented voice.

'What is this all for?' Emma asked as she was surrounded by people preening and prodding her.

'There's a woman who died two days ago. A friend of mine. Her death hasn't been reported to the Space Bureau, so you're going to pretend to be her.'

Looking at the photo shown her, Emma saw the friend was a beauty of Vivian Leigh calibre. Her confidence instantly took a dive but the woman, who seemed to be some kind of beautician, set about doing her make-up.

While this was going on, the three men were busy contacting various people.

'We're leaving in three hours, on the last flight out of the spaceport.'

'If our party is just Meelians, we should be okay. Although if they find out about her,' he nodded toward Emma, 'it could mean trouble.'

'But if all the Meelians from the Tokyo area just up and vanish, they'll get suspicious, no? All the Meelians on Earth are going to head home within the month, after all.'

'If that's what you're worried about, I think our story about a seven-yearly pilgrimage should cover us. We're also carrying out historical research, so the Terran government can hardly complain. The real trouble will occur when we get back to Meele.'

'Yes, because none of the returnees have any intention of ever coming back to Earth. The Terran government might not like it, but they can hardly use that as a reason for starting an interplanetary war. The other planets wouldn't stand for it.'

'You say that, but the other planets have their own interests, and that complicates things.'

Emma was given Meelian-style clothes to put on.

'Ooh, it's Marianne *de ma Jeunesse*! Although the proportions are somewhat off,' Sol said, making a theatrical gesture.

The screening process at the spaceport went smoothly. 'That's because they're just temps,' Jebba explained to Emma. 'The regular employees are off with stomach complaints . . . They ate too much Mirinnian wild beef.'

'You're such a schemer, Jebba,' Sol chipped in.

'This is all for the sake of your grand old love story, Sol. One in Tokyo, one in Ginza . . .' Jebba broke into the lyrics from an old song. There was barely anyone in the spaceport. Sol put a cigarette to his lips, shoved his hands in his pockets and began spouting excuses: 'I'm telling you, it's not like that.'

'What line are we flying with? World New Space? Or Stardust Space Service?' Emma asked quietly.

'No, not one of the big ones. We're taking Meele Space Line.' Sol tossed away his final pack of cigarettes with a regretful expression.

'Thank goodness. At least the captain and the engineer will be Meelians. I was afraid you were planning to space-jack the flight midway.'

'If we did that, we'd be playing straight into Earth's hands. I looked up the passenger list and was surprised to see Terrans on there, but it turns out they've all got some Meelian blood. It's tough to get onto Meele these days. There are only two Terran groups that can get in: the Scientific Investigation Commission, which charters its own flights, and an agricultural products company. But even with them, there are just a very few Terrans in the upper ranks. The rest of the workers are people from other planets, like us.'

Anxiety rose up in Emma. She took Sol's arm and made to ask him something.

'Time to go.' Glancing at the information screen, Sol patted her back, urging her forward. The announcement resonated across the empty waiting room. Around them, green-faced people slowly got to their feet and made their way over to the beltway entrance.

'This is my first time on a spaceship,' Emma said. 'I've never even been to Mars. My sister went to Kamiroi on her honeymoon, though.'

'Oh yeah?'

Sol seemed absorbed in his own thoughts. This was nothing new for him, but in this moment Emma found it particularly distressing. She squeezed his arm harder.

In front of them the huge silver form of the spaceship came into view.

And so began life in the cabin with a low cream ceiling. Emma was sharing a room with Sol, but he was always off doing something. On the rare occasions he did return to the cabin, he'd quickly disengage. Their conversations were fragmentary, and she had the feeling that he was trying to evade her in some way. At mealtimes, her meals, and hers alone, would be brought to her room on a tray like the ones used in hospitals.

'I can't do anything about it. I have to eat with the others in the canteen so we can hatch our plans and talk over all the possibilities,' Sol explained patiently, squeezing her hand.

'But I'm the only one who's being excluded. I know it's because I'm a Terran.'

Beyond the reaches of Emma's understanding, a complex situation was unfolding – and Sol was concealing it from her.

'I wish I'd never met you. I've left my family and my home behind me, and all you do is ostracize me.'

'Not this again. Please try and understand my position.'

'And how am I supposed to do that? There's no way of understanding it when I've no clue what's going on!'

'Look, I understand that you're angry because you're cooped up all alone here. But we can't let you go walking around. There are also their feelings to consider.'

'I'm not well, Sol. I feel like I'm going mad.'

If only Sol would look her in the eye when he was talking to her. He'd begun to lose weight and had become lethargic, his eyes alone hinting at his old energy with a glint of intense colour. He reminded her of a dragonfly. Was he eating properly? Was he not getting enough sleep?

'I find it hard to breathe, Sol. I've no appetite, and I feel dizzy all the time. Symptoms this bad can't just be a matter of a change in environment. I don't think it's a question of the food not agreeing with me, either. Is there something in the food here? Some kind of drug?'

Sol continued to stare at the wall. She went to touch his shoulder but then felt, instinctively, that she shouldn't. His face in profile looked unspeakably depressed.

'I'll send for a doctor,' he said after a while, his voice gravelly.

'Are we still not there yet? How much longer will it take?'

'The ship's pilot isn't very good at navigating the warps. He got his licence over thirty years ago.' He turned to look at her and smiled.

'What are you hiding, Sol? What's happened?' She reached out and touched his shoulder.

'I'm not hiding anything!' Sol roared. She saw a muscle in his cheek spasm. His eyes narrowed and blazed with a violent green light. His white face looked like it was made of plastic.

'I'm sick of this! I want to go back to Earth!' Emma cried, her voice faltering.

'Go back then! Right now! Get them to send out a rescue rocket.'

Sol's face was blanched to transparency. Emma stood up, making to push past him and leave the room. At the very last moment, Sol's arm flew out and knocked her down. Emma registered the blow to her forehead and then came the pain. Sol squeezed the fist he'd used to punch her with his other hand.

'Don't make a fuss,' he said in a strangely restrained voice. 'If you can't trust me, then forgive me. But even if you can't do that, you can't just give up.' His voice had regained its usual composure. He sounded sad. 'You mustn't forget, Emma. I'll never forget how you were when I first met you, and all the things that've happened since. Why do you think it is that we haven't had a war on my planet for two millennia? It's because we *don't* forget. We don't forget the fear or the tragedy. When feelings like that are powerful enough, they get into our genes – just a small amount, but that's all it takes. When an emotion's sufficiently strong, we can't ever forget about it.'

Emma pressed a hand to the lump already forming on her forehead.

'Does it hurt?' Sol said, drawing closer and touching her face.

'Yes.'

'Why do you forget things so quickly? Meelians could never look back on war with nostalgia – nationalistic, planetary or otherwise. Our feelings don't change or get eroded over time. And so when we reach a certain age – it differs from person to person, but when that person's mental capacity reaches its capacity, it means their time has come.'

Now Sol was looking her straight in the eye, speaking in a voice that was almost a whisper as if he were trying to soothe her to sleep. She could smell his breath.

'Will that happen to you too, Sol?' She looked away from him.

'Yes.'

'When? You're not trying to tell me that your time is coming?'

'I can't say. Even if I knew, I couldn't tell anyone,' he said. He seemed to be suffering.

'Are there some people who tell others?'

'I suppose.'

Silence reigned between them. The cabin had no windows, so there was no looking out at the stars outside. How much more of this would she have to endure – this confinement for reasons she didn't even understand? The cream ceiling seemed to get lower all the time.

Emma could hear the faint growl of an engine. Was that the ship's computer? There would be no returning to Earth, Emma thought to herself.

'I'm exhausted.'

She went back to bed. She had all the time in the world to sleep. That was all she did of late. Every day she grew thinner and frailer; every day more of her physical strength deserted her.

'Tomorrow we're going to get married,' Sol said as he left the room.

Emma felt so despondent she didn't know what to do with herself. It seemed as though she was falling into a fathomless dark pit. It took everything she had to crawl out of bed.

For her wedding, Emma didn't change out of her indoor spacesuit. She felt terrible for the duration of the ceremony. She understood that she and Sol were marrying solely in order to procure the paperwork that would allow her to enter Meele. But she didn't want to be tied to Sol at an unhappy time like this. She felt she'd been dragged into marriage.

When it was over, Emma returned to bed and was given medicine and an injection. I'm going to die soon, she thought. It's possible I'm being used as a guinea pig here.

Jebba appeared in her room. 'How are you feeling?'

'Awful.' It was an effort to speak, and her voice came out raspy.

'You're not happy?' he asked solicitously.

'As if I could be happy! I never imagined that marrying Sol could make me feel this awful. I know that this is all part of some *plot*.' She shot Jebba a piercing glance.

'You shouldn't talk too much, you'll tire yourself out.'

'Do you think I care? I'm going to die soon anyway. I'll talk all I want. You can all fuck off and die! There'll be plenty of time for your goddamn reasoning then!'

'Look, the Terran government went and announced that the Space Bureau director's sister has been abducted by Meelians. We had to carry out a wedding ceremony to show it was consensual. But the Earth side won't believe it, anyway. They're going to say you've been blackmailed or you agreed while under the influence of drugs. Of course it's not like they actually believe these things, but that's the message.'

'None of that matters to me.'

185

Emma was feeling utterly desperate. How miserable it would be to breathe her last in a spaceship like this one!

'And they're pinning another crime on Sol as well. Do you know Luana? She was killed two days before we left.'

'Oh, I wouldn't be surprised Sol did it,' Emma wailed.

Sol chose this moment to enter the room.

Emma glared at him, eyes full of malice. Jebba took his leave, and Sol sat down in the chair, his eyes glinting as they turned on her.

The noise of the computer was joined by a different dull thumping sound, resonating all around the room. Sol sat there, saying nothing.

'So you're being charged with murder? That's just great.' Emma said, coughing. She even managed a faint smile.

'You think so, do you?' His face was a strange shade, as if he was feverish.

'I don't know what you did to Luana, but I know that you're gradually killing me.'

She was out of breath. It hurt.

'Why do you think that? Why would I have brought you along if I planned to do such a thing?'

'You've diverged from your original plan. Things have happened that you never predicted. Besides, the people from your planet hate me. I'm not needed. I'm excess baggage.'

Emma was now totally convinced that something toxic was being mixed in with her meals and medicine. And Sol was letting it all happen. It was now beyond her to try and think about things from his perspective or about how he might be feeling.

'This is probably the last time I'll come to see you,' he said suddenly.

Summoning all the strength she had, Emma sat up.

'Has your time come?'

'I don't know.'

The air between them was stifling. Emma switched on the radio. Even if they couldn't pick up any broadcasts from Earth, they might be able to tune in to a relay station or the Spaceship Broadcasting Corporation's pirate reports.

There was no news on the radio – it was all music. 'Love Potion No. 9' began wafting through the empty space.

'So, this week is sixties week! We've been flooded with so many great listener requests, I want to play them all. Next up is "Satisfaction". You all heard this one, by any chance? It's by a group called the Rolling Stones . . .'

'I can't get no satisfaction . . .' Emma sang along weakly with Mick Jagger. Almost immediately, she felt out of breath. I'm going to die, she thought, and soon.

'Okay, and next up is . . . What the . . .? Bessie Smith? Look, first off that's the wrong decade, and just because something's old doesn't make it good, you hear? I hate to see the evening sun go down, says old Bessie. Oh well, I don't care, maybe I'll play it anyway. Man, I'm definitely going to be out of a job . . .'

The disk jockey's chirpy monologue continued for a while, then 'St Louis Blues' came on, but it wasn't Bessie Smith singing.

'You said you'd never forget. Is that still true?' Emma said.

'Forget what?'

187

Sol's eyes were hollow. He could easily have been a patient in a psychiatric ward.

'What happened between us. The things you said.'

Sun Ra's 'Heliocentric' came on. This playlist is all over the place, Emma thought, and snapped off the radio.

Sol stretched out his neck and looked at Emma with an expression she'd never seen before, one she found impossible to read.

'Or have you forgotten after all?'

Silence tumbled in on them like water flooding the room. Sol remained silent.

'Say it!' Emma said, her voice forceful.

'I've forgotten,' Sol said. A burst of clamorous modern jazz went spiralling around in Emma's head. She let out a long sigh and dropped her hand to her side.

That night, Sol's last thoughts entered Emma's consciousness. And come the morning, he was gone.

There was no intergalactic war, just a minor skirmish. Six months later, Meele became a colony of Earth.

TERMINAL BOREDOM

HE was standing on the other side of the turnstiles. Duded-up as always in some ill-fitting clothes that all probably belonged to HIS dad. The trousers in particular were way too baggy. HE gave a little wave with one hand, not even bothering to peel HIS back off the pillar HE was leaning against.

I inserted my ticket into the slot and waited for the metal bar to move out of the way. The boy behind me plastered himself to my back and followed me through. He probably couldn't afford a ticket. Once we were on the other side, he mumbled something that might have been 'Thanks' and slouched off.

'What was that?' HE asked, smirking.

'Same thing you always do.'

'All the heads who couldn't make it through are grouping up.'

'What'll they do? If they miss the last train, I mean.'

'Just get thrown out.'

'Yeah? I thought they could spend the night if they didn't have anyone to vouch for them.'

'That's ancient history. The population's got too big, they can't accommodate everyone anymore.'

We leaned against the pillar side by side. My legs got tired pretty much right away, though, and I got down on my haunches.

HE crouched down beside me. 'Wanna go somewhere?'

I sighed. 'Sure . . . Aboveground, I guess?'

HE sighed too. Then, with an exaggerated air: 'We do the same thing every time we hang out. I thought we were supposed to be madly in love.'

I rolled my eyes. We were similar, that's all it ever was. Two years ago I'd been happy about it. Not only did we have the same sign and the same blood type, but we were even the same height and weight. Now I'm an inch taller, though.

'Good grief.' HE stood up. 'Even moving around like this, I feel like I'm gonna drop dead. Why do I feel so sluggish?'

'Have you eaten?'

'Oh, there you go. Slipped my mind.'

'I've been trying to eat before I go out. I keep on collapsing. You need to eat a couple of times a day, apparently.'

'I wonder why,' HE mused vacantly. I had always assumed HE was doing an impression of a moron, but sometimes I wonder if HE isn't simply stupid.

'It's probably the boredom. If you're not doing anything . . .'

'Yeah. You must be right.'

There were a bunch of young men and women (aged from twelve or thirteen all the way up to thirty or so) sitting around next to the stairwell up to the surface. Not a job between them.

190

'How about we head to the unemployment cafeteria?' HE suggested over HIS shoulder.

'No way. That's where all the gangsters hang out. If they snatch my ID card, I'm screwed. They'll sell it on the black market.'

'But you've got me to protect you.' HE burst out laughing. I gave HIM a look that made it clear I wasn't amused.

Aboveground, the sun was beating down on the filthy town spread out before us. Unfettered spaces scare me. I'm not used to scenes that aren't in a frame. Looking at a picture inside a border always calms me down, whether it's an ultravista or the real thing. It's probably from all the TV.

'Maybe I'll do a little shopping.'

'I don't want to be involved. I'll wait outside.'

'It's more fun with a co-conspirator. Maybe not you, though, you seem like you'd blow it spectacularly.'

HE prides himself on the fact that HE's never been caught shoplifting. HE tells me the trick is to target the security cameras' blind spots.

Walking towards the plaza, the one with the fountain, HE scoped out the stores lining either side of the street. Abruptly HE turned into a pharmacy. I just kept on strolling along. HE caught up to me again almost right away. After walking in silence for a little while, HE turned into a small alley. Probably going to see HIS fence.

After a minute or two HE came down from the second floor of a building with some cash in HIS hand. It wasn't much. 'Here,' HE gave it to me. 'Not my best work. The clerk was super intense, he was giving me the eye the whole time. Probably didn't want to lose his job. So I had to settle for stuff that wasn't worth a whole lot.'

HE took a tiny box out of HIS pocket and showed it to me.

'What's that?'

'Some kind of after-the-fact contraception, apparently. I've never needed it, so I didn't know what it was. My fence explained it to me.'

'I wonder who uses it.'

'People who do it a lot, or who have a lot of sperm on account of some weird metabolic quirk. Elderly perverts, probably. What's wrong?'

'Struggling to remember the last time I did it . . .'

'If it was with me, we did it two years ago when we first met.'

'So we did.'

'Have you done it with someone else since?'

'Come on, how often do you think I can do something like that? It's exhausting.'

'Sure, but . . . tiring yourself out isn't so bad. You get that feeling of having really *done* something. Don't you think it's dull never wearing yourself out at all?'

'Dunno.'

It seemed like something we ought to do. Might be that's why we broke up for a year or so. We didn't do it for such a long time that we started to lose 'that loving feeling'. We were only seeing each other now because HE had appeared on television; my mother was one of the execs at the company that produced the programme. It was some staged show called *The Psychoanalysis Room* or something. When I called HIM and asked why HE'd gone on the show, *he* said, 'I thought maybe if my mum saw it, she'd take pity and come find me.' But there was no way HIS mother, who had vanished into thin air fifteen years ago, was ever going to recognize her son. HE was twenty-one years old now and appearing under an alias. That's what I thought, anyway, but I didn't say it out loud.

We went into a fast food joint. It proclaimed itself a 'Gourmet Soupery'. What was gourmet about it, I couldn't tell you. I got a little dizzy when I tried to lift the tray with our two bowls on it. Despite chiding HIM about HIS diet earlier, I realized I hadn't eaten anything since yesterday myself. They were saying on the news that more and more young people were forgetting to eat, starving to death.

'This feels kind of embarrassing somehow,' I said as I picked up my spoon.

'Uh-huh.' HE nodded.

'I've never eaten with someone else before.'

'Me neither.'

We ate sitting side by side, gazing at the video screen. It's so hard to relax without something to look at. The screen was showing a sunset over some southern island. The camera didn't move, so it was pretty much like an ultravista. Once the sun had sunk fully behind the horizon, the programme changed to *Top Forty This Week*. That restaurant chain's catchphrase is 'Brand new videos, guaranteed.'

I stacked the bowls one inside the other and put them into the nearby bin.

'How's your girlfriend?'

'Hm?'

'The girl you were going out with after me.'

'Haven't seen her.'

'How come?'

HE furrowed HIS brow, then let out a sigh as if to say *guess I've got no choice*. 'Her parents are still together.'

'Don't hear that too often.'

'Maybe it's that, or maybe it's something else, but she has total faith in society. She's so boisterous, always got too much energy . . . Hell, she's even got aspirations.'

'To marry you?'

'To have children and stuff.'

'Through IVF?'

'Yeah. Not likely, right? Not with a physique like that.'

She was about 4' 9" and 110 pounds. The average height for someone that weight is about 5' 6", men and women alike.

'Anyway, that's all I'm gonna say about it.' Sighing again, HE returned HIS gaze to the screen.

What more could there be to say? Maybe she still had periods. I used to myself for two or three years when I was younger. Once I hit eighteen I started eating less and less, and then before I knew it I just wasn't getting them anymore. I mean, no one's going to like you if you have a classic woman's figure (or a man's). The only ones with any meat on their bones in this day and age are older people and pregnant women on a hospital diet.

HE was staring at the pop star on the screen. She was probably the one HE was truly in love with. I've got my own favourite celebrity as well, so I'm well aware that there's no point in being jealous. It's just an image, it's not real—how can you compete with that? And, yet, the jealousy is there.

'Did you vote for her in the last election?' I mean, I had to be jealous, didn't I? Since we're still treating what we had (HIM and me) as a love affair. The instant I became aware of this sense of obligation, it started to feel stupid.

'Yeah. So what?'

'It's idiotic, giving people the right to vote at the age of fifteen.'

'Maybe so.'

'And all this *Let the future shine! The Number Whatever Election* bullshit.'

'Voter turnout's gone up, though. Now that all you have to do is sit in front of your TV and press a button for your favourite celeb.'

'But they don't even publicly announce which politicians the celebrity delegates choose with the votes they get.'

'No shit, Sherlock.' HE shook HIS head. 'Let's get outta here.'

The streets were overflowing with the jobless. Sitting, standing, talking, strumming guitars.

'How come there're so many, I wonder.' HIS mood seemed to have improved.

'It's Shinjuku.'

'Why do they all gather in the same place, though. Even when they have to dodge the fare to get here.'

'They come for the spectacle. To check each other out.'

The closer we got to the Koma Theater, the more of them there were. Two police patrol ships were flying overhead. They would periodically descend and play the same taped message over their loudspeakers: *It is against the law to remain in the same place for more than twenty minutes. Please move along.*

We got to the plaza and sat down side by side.

'So what's up?' HE asked. There was nothing much else to talk about.

'Nothing at all.' I instantly started to get irritated.

'Doing well?'

'Well enough.'

'How's your mother?'

'Good.' How the hell did I get stuck with this moron? 'You?'

'Me? Yeah, I'm good.'

'How's your father?'

'Lately it's as though he's just hit puberty.' HE smiled faintly. 'Spends a lot of time lost in thought.'

'About what?'

'I dunno, maybe he's having a midlife crisis. Turning sixty and all.' We both laughed. 'No, seriously though, seems like he's found love,' HE added. 'Old people have so much energy, you know? It seems like he's really giving it everything he's got. Keeping a diary, writing letters, sending gifts.'

'Is she a real person?' A strange question, but HE seemed to know what I meant. Not a celebrity, in other words.

'I think so, yeah. Doesn't seem like a green door, anyway.'

An image, HE meant. Though it's a term they use with psychedelics, too.

'Isn't that a lot of effort? Being in love at that age?'

'Yeah. They act like it's this huge deal. Not like *us*, right? Young people get involved out of a sense of obligation. It's like we have to. Or because we've got nothing better to do.' HE

196

followed this with some total bullshit: 'I'm not talking about you, of course. *You're* special. You understand that, don't you?'

'And?' I looked down my nose at HIM. I couldn't tell whether I was genuinely pissed off or not. The performance had just become a part of my personality. If nothing else, I can be pretty sure I'm not happy, I thought vacantly.

'You know I care about you, right?' HIS voice had developed an edge to it. Though maybe that was an act as well.

'Like how?' Not that I really cared.

'All kinds of ways—'

You, in the black, move along. The warning sounded over the loudspeaker of the patrol ship. *Move along.*

As the vehicle started to descend, the figure in black leapt up and took off running. Not swiftly enough, though. A mechanical arm reached down out of the patrol ship. The perp raised both hands. If you've got your arms at your sides when they grab you, they get pinned there and you're more likely to get injured. The patrol ship departed with the black-clad figure dangling helplessly in the air beneath it.

'Fucking horrible.' HE looked up.

'What'll happen now?'

'A formal warning, and a fine.'

'You've been arrested before, right?'

'Once. The cops will make an example of you whenever they feel like it. They can always find something to charge you with afterwards.'

'How did it feel?'

'Being carried up and away with my arms spread out like that . . . It reminded me of the opening to that Fellini movie.'

197

Meant nothing to me.

'You don't know much of anything, do you. No wonder you can't hold down a job.'

Once every six months we have to sit for the employment examination. It gets recorded on our ID cards. What the penalty is for not showing up, I don't know.

'I pass the exam every time,' I protested half-heartedly.

'And? What occupation category do they give you?'

'Waitress. There're requirements for that too, you know. Height, for example. Your *girlfriend* couldn't get that job.'

'That girl's always getting engaged, just so she doesn't have to take the employment exam. They allow a certain period for marriage preparations. This conversation's going in circles. What a drag.'

'Were you two engaged?'

'I don't want to say.'

Then they must've been.

I started chewing a fingernail. HE took that hand in HIS and squeezed it gently. 'Quit being such a pill. It's a real turn-off.'

I remained stubbornly silent.

'OK then, who was that call from that one time?' HE asked.

'Gimme a break. What are you even talking about?'

'You got a phone call that time we went to your place together. You didn't put it on screen because it was a man, right?'

'The caller had the picture switched off, that's all.'

'Who the hell does that?'

'Plenty of people. I do it all the time myself. When I'm not feeling presentable, for instance.'

What a nightmare.

'And when would that be?'

'Like when I've got bedhead.'

'You always keep the picture switched on when it's me. Even when your hair isn't done.'

'That's because it's you.'

I want to go home. Alone.

'And you always wanted to get rid of me right after.'

'You're imagining things.'

How do I wrap this up?

'You want to go home, don't you? Because I'm asking all these questions.'

A series of dull thuds sounded behind us. A man was hitting a woman over the head with something heavy and hard. Again and again. The woman had her hands up. We heard one final scream. She collapsed. Covered in blood.

The woman wasn't moving. Her attacker was muttering something under his breath. *Serves you right . . . That's what you get for . . .* that kind of thing.

The man started to walk away, not even bothering to wipe away the blood spattered all over him. No one could move. The patrol ship didn't arrive for another two minutes.

I thought HE might faint. HE's anaemic, and HIS already-pale face had gone white as a sheet.

'It's so . . . vivid.' HE was gazing at the bloody aftermath of the attack.

'Let's get out of here.'

'Hold on a sec. That was so intense, I was rooted to the spot. Almost like it was the real thing.'

'It *was* real.'

'Yeah?' HE stepped closer to inhale the scent of blood, but the cops shooed HIM away. It was a pose anyway. HE has virtually no sense of smell. Can't smell or taste much of anything. I'm the same way. Maybe that's why kids nowadays don't care about eating. And why our everyday lives feel like a scene from a TV show.

'I end up putting a frame around everything I see,' HE murmured, seemingly to himself. 'It makes it seem fresh, helps me relax as a viewer.' Then HE turned to me and grinned (at least I think it was a grin). 'Man, I haven't felt this amped in ages. That really wasn't staged, huh. Where are the TV cameras? I want my mum to see this.'

I kept silent. I can't explain it clearly, but I had the sense that HE was on the verge of some kind of mental breakdown.

The TV cameras never showed up.

But there was a thirtyish man taking an (amateur) video of the scene.

'I'm gonna go ask him.' HE was back to HIS usual cheerful self. 'For what?'

'A copy.'

There was a sound from the front hall. 'What a racket,' I thought, trying to focus my attention on the screen; I was watching *Gone with the Wind*. Seemed like my mother had arrived home, and right at the finale – the scene where Rhett Butler leaves and Scarlett O'Hara collapses on the stairs. I always end up crying at that part. No matter how many times I watch it, I end up crying.

Ever since I've been old enough to really understand the world (these past two years or so), I've never once cried at a scene in real life. Whenever something serious happens, I just convince myself it's no big deal. I do my best to avoid any kind of shock. I've been fooling myself this way for long enough that it's become a habit, and now nothing affects me. But in the world of make-believe, I can still relax enough to let flow my tears.

I heard my mother go into her room.

I wept buckets and pondered Scarlett's fate. Would it be possible for her to win back Rhett's love? No, I have a feeling he's the kind of man who never changes his mind once it's made up. Not like the softies I'd always dated. The kind of men you see in the movies would be hard to handle in real life, though – they're so fixated on their own masculinity. And sometimes that male pride, that proper behaviour, it all starts to seem ridiculous. If they could just get over themselves, then everything might be a whole lot simpler.

I pressed the button and the screen went black.

'Doing OK?' My mother came into the room with a box of tissue paper in one hand, removing her make-up.

'Yeah, you know, I'm fine, thanks.' I felt awkward, like I didn't know what to say. I always get that way when I'm talking with my mother.

'What have you been up to lately? Anything interesting going on?'

I couldn't just dismiss her attempts at conversation.

'Same as usual. I did the housework and now I'm just vegging out.'

'Hmm, must be nice to have so much time on your hands.' My mother was crouching down and spreading cream all over her face. I had no desire to see a grown woman looking like that.

'If you check the memory you'll see, but . . . There was a phone call from Daddy.' This was a dicey topic.

'I see.' My mother's expression didn't change. But her face was a mask of white so it was hard to tell. 'What did he say?'

'I recorded it . . . Wasn't much of a conversation, though. I just can't get on the same wavelength as someone like him. I know he means well, but . . .'

'He sucks all the air out of the room, that man.'

Was I allowed to agree?

'And every word out of his mouth is an exaggeration.' My mother nodded to herself. The cream had become translucent. She gestured for the tissues and started wiping it away. 'That's what they used to call "personality" back in the last century. I hate these wishy-washy boys nowadays, but that doesn't mean I want someone so hard-headed.'

'Doesn't it kind of seem like he wants you back?' I couldn't settle down with the TV off. But I felt like it'd be rude to turn it on.

'Is that the impression you got?'

'Yeah.'

'Still as dumb as ever!' Her former husband, she meant. 'He's like a wind-up metal robot, he'll keep on going just as he is till Judgement Day.'

'Mum.'

'What?'

'You know a lot of words, huh.'

'That's because I don't spend all day in front of the tube like you. I even read books, if you can believe it.'

By the time she was done wiping off her face, there was a huge mound of used tissues. I threw them away.

'There was a call from Daddy's wife, too. Later on.'

'What did she say?' My mother stood up with the tissue box in her hand.

'She just kept squawking on and on, asking, *Has my husband been over there* – she's a real dog, huh.'

I was buttering my mother up. She's the one who provides for me, after all. I feel like I have to do something for her. HE also comes from a single-parent home, but HE approaches it differently. HE's decided it was HIS father's fault that HIS mother left, so HE deals with it by bleeding him dry and ignoring him at the same time. Angelic trumpets will herald the day of HIS mother's return. HE seems to see it as the day of HIS salvation, in every possible sense. That day will never come, of course, so HE can make HIS fantasy as grandiose as HE likes.

'You think I'm prettier?' my mother asked, her face gleaming.

'Of course I do. I mean, she's short and fat, and swarthy. And she's got that raspy voice.' While I was offering this up for my mother's benefit, it struck me how similar Daddy's new wife was to that girl HE had been engaged to. It wasn't a question of whether they actually resembled one another. As long as my image of them was the same, I could lump them into the same category. Spurred on by this realization, my tone grew more forceful. 'And having four kids? Giving birth to them naturally? What is she, an animal?'

My mother was clearly pleased. She's the kind of person who always wants to be number one. She was saying something about how a lot of cats were infertile lately. 'Come in here and let's have a chat.' She went into her room.

Is it really that important for parents and children to talk to each other? TV dramas are always talking about it, so maybe it is.

My mother had finished tending to her face and was lying on her belly on the bed, smoking a cigarette. It's a vice she didn't want anyone to know about.

I sat down in the chair next to the bed and clasped my hands around my knee.

'It has to do with work.'

I nodded, to show that I was listening.

'You're aware that if you stimulate a certain part of the brain, it produces a sense of euphoria, right?'

I wasn't, but I nodded anyway.

'Such experiments were first conducted a long time ago. They would hook a patient up with electrodes and have them flip a switch five thousand times an hour. Now they have a device that links the subject directly to a television. When the monitor is turned on, it begins to stimulate the brain. The subject no longer has to flip the switch each time; instead, a weak electrical current is transmitted automatically at appropriate intervals.'

'I've heard about that. One of my friends was using it.' She was a real space cadet, though, and it's not clear if she was always that way or if it was just thanks to the electrode attached to her brain.

'But it hasn't caught on, has it.'

'Do you have to have surgery?'

'A very simple procedure. Quick and painless. Like getting your ear pierced.' For some reason my mother was angry. Or so it seemed.

'And then?' I felt like I had to say something, so I kept going. 'You feel good? As long as you're watching TV?'

'Probably.'

'Then, wouldn't you just watch TV all day long?' As if that wasn't what I did already. When I'm alone in my room, I'm mostly watching TV. And I'm alone in my room most of the time.

'They're mounting a huge campaign this time, trying to encourage people to get the device installed. Personally, I'm against it.'

Was she speaking as a mother?

'How come?'

'I worry about going to such lengths to try and get people to watch more TV.'

'But they're committed to it now, right?'

'They're in production as we speak. Five-second and fifteen-second versions. The ad copy makes my skin crawl, too. *Feel Good*, and *Happiness is within your reach* – that kind of thing. Feels obscene somehow, don't you think?'

'Like commercials for gravestones.' I said the first thing that popped into my head.

'Now that you mention it, sure. Hell is keeping a low profile these days, and the whole country is under the spell of this image of Heaven. The difference, though, is that with Hell at least you know what you're getting. But with Heaven, everything's ambiguous. There are no actively good feelings, just a passive, ambiguous contentment.'

What's wrong with that? I didn't get why she thought that sounded so terrible.

'But it's good for you work-wise, right?'

'It certainly is.'

'I'm sure it'll be a hit.'

I'm a sucker for trends. I don't have much in the way of agency. I always want to try whatever's popular.

'If you become a TV addict, though, you won't be able to do anything else.'

I pretended to think hard about this. 'But, there's nothing else to do.'

'Oh? Really? What do you do all day while I'm at work?'

'It's not like I get up at the same time every day. But usually sometime before noon. First off, I have something to drink, you know. Then I watch TV. And I slowly start to feel human again. I take a bath. After that I clean the house. You see, I can't really move my body until I've had a nice hot soak. Laundry. The housework only takes about an hour altogether. After all that, it's TV for the rest of the day.' I really *don't* do anything at all. Even I was taken aback.

'That's it?'

What, did my mother think I was studying or something?

'I'm unemployed, so I've got no money. It's not like I can go out anywhere.'

'What about the library?'

'They only have the mainstream stuff, books and videos both. The other day I went to take out *Blade Runner* but they didn't even have *that*. I couldn't believe it. Going over to a friend's place doesn't cost anything, but talking to other people is so exhausting. I don't see my friends all that often, so it's hard to tell how to act. And talking to Daddy is exhausting for different reasons.' Talking with my mother like this was exhausting too. I'm just no good with living, breathing human beings.

'You can't find work at all?' My mother sounded concerned about me.

'. . . Uh-uh.'

It's because I'm stupid and childish, I thought. Each occupational category has a designated minimum IQ. Most require a higher ability index than mine. There are too many people, so no wonder. Then there are the ones like HIM, who are intelligent but fail the exam on purpose, who want their parents to take care of them forever. Of course, HE also does it to exact revenge on HIS father.

'Now why would that be, I wonder.'

'Mama, can I say something weird?'

'Of course.'

'Bad luck seems to follow me around. It sucks for me personally that I always get fired after a couple of weeks and never make any money, but the businesses themselves always seem to fall on hard times too. From the day I start working somewhere, the customers just stop showing up . . . I've started to feel like it's somehow my fault for even putting on a professional act and going to work. It's like I'm causing trouble for everyone.'

'You're imagining things.'

207

My mother smiled. How could she be so sure? I wish I had the confidence to make pronouncements like that. Does it come from her devotion to her work?

'Bring me some water, dear.' My mother shook out her hair.

Going into the kitchen, I let out a sigh. I'm a real sigher, but I do my best to hold it in until I'm alone. That's part of the reason it's so hard for me to be around other people. When I'm with HIM, I can sigh. Maybe that's why I put up with HIM.

'Why don't you go back to school?' my mother asked when I brought her the water.

'It's not like there are a lot of places I *can* go.'

After middle school, I went to a design school that didn't have an entrance exam. They didn't take attendance either. They had some fancy ideal of a 'liberal education'. It was fun. Even after I graduated, I would still go hang out there whenever I got an invite to a dance party or something. That's where I met HIM. I liked that HE wasn't an old classmate of mine. Still, it's not like it had to be HIM. Anyone who was about the same height as me and was similarly skinny and androgynous would've done just as well. And that place was chock full of guys like that.

'Well, you don't need to worry about money, at least. I'm in the top income bracket.'

'I know that – is it OK if I go now?'

'Go ahead.' My mother reached out and began adjusting her sleep dial.

I went to my room instead of back to the couch. I opened up the TV guide and looked through it. There are so many lines and it takes a fair amount of time. Got to be thorough, though – I almost didn't notice that one of my favourite bands was on.

I hurriedly turned on the TV.

I think Yūki (that's the singer) is cute and smart and great. Though I've been upset about a daytime show I saw where they revealed he had a lover.

Nothing eases the boredom, of course. Aside from maybe when a pop star I've decided I like is on. It's not that I like the content of the programming itself. So much of it is total trash. I just enjoy the feeling of sitting there spacing out in front of the TV set. Because I don't have to be active. Doing anything of my own volition is so painful that I can't handle it. If I can just avoid that pain, that's enough for me.

I wanted to crank up the volume, so I put on my headphones. The shows would keep on coming forever. I slowly began to slip into a world all my own.

My father committed suicide.

I have no idea what went on between my parents. My mother has taken a leave of absence from work and checked herself into one of those mental hospitals that sells itself like a resort. Apparently she's going to write an essay on the world of television while she's there.

The worst part about it is that my dad's wife has started calling all the time. If someone grabs my hand when I don't want them to, I can never bring myself to shake them off. That's just the kind of person I am. So all I can do when this person, the wife of someone who was basically a total stranger to me, calls up is grit my teeth and listen to her reminisce and lament.

'Do you have any idea how hopelessly in love with him I was?' What the hell am I supposed to say to that? So I just keep silent. It's not like I can tell her I thought my father was a loser.

I know perfectly well what a good match my father and his new wife were. They both had total faith in society. Which is I guess why he committed suicide – he actually believed his death might have some kind of effect. Talk about optimistic.

At the same time, I've developed a conditioned response to the face of my father's widow: every time I see it, I'm reminded of that girl HE was with. I've become crazed with jealousy. Feels like the first time in forever I've felt any kind of emotion. Having emotions is a good thing. Better than not having them, anyway.

'Why do you have the video switched off?' HE asked from the screen.

'Because I'm naked,' I lied. I felt like messing with HIS head a little.

'Can you put something on? It makes me anxious when I can't see your face.'

'I've got nothing to wear,' I replied, suppressing a giggle.

'. . . Fine. I'll turn mine off too.' The screen went black.

'So what's up?' Having a conversation with just our voices was strange, but kind of fun.

'I've got *something important* to ask you, so can you get serious?'

'Sure.'

'Man, this is embarrassing. I'm not sure about asking this – should I do it anyway, even though I can't see your face?'

What a weirdo.

'Just spit it out.'

'OK then – do you like me?'

'Sure I like you. You know that.'

'Like how?'

'Like I like myself.'

'That's one hell of an answer.'

'What's this about?'

'Well, I've got this plan – is this conversation being recorded?'

'Nope.'

'You sure?'

'I hate holding on to love letters. What's up with you anyway?'

'Well, I mean, I was thinking, what if we became one, like, body and soul. What d'you think?'

'I have no idea what you mean.' What could HE possibly have in mind?

'I got one of those devices installed in my brain. I want you to try it too. It'll change your whole outlook.'

'Maybe. But my mum's against it. She's away right now, but she'd never give me the money for it anyway.'

'I want you to get one more than anything. If you don't, we can never become true mirror images.'

'What happens when you get it?'

'All the shitty stuff stops bothering you. Like, you realize that there's a simple way of dealing with everything that's been weighing on you up till now. You can just tack on an illogical ending to the story, like a deus ex machina for life. Reality feels like a TV show, and TV shows feel like reality. It's like the boundary between them breaks down, like you're living in a dream.'

'Sounds like my kind of world. But I'd prefer living in a nightmare.'

'It does cause a little bit of confusion. Sometimes you have to think for a minute before you can be sure if something's happened to you or to the protagonist of a TV show. But that's no big deal, right?'

'Not at all,' I answered right away. TV show, reality, who cares? Comfort, feeling good, that's all that matters. And I almost never get to feel that way. I'm always just . . . bored.

'Okay, so when you get one, you feel good? Comfortable?'

'Yup. I think it has something to do with endorphins. The other day my tooth hurt so bad I could barely think, but once I turned the TV on, it went away.'

'En-what-now?'

'Opioids in your brain. Apparently if you keep jogging consistently for more than eight weeks, your brain suddenly starts producing tons of them. Daddy told me running makes him feel so good that he can't give it up. He's away on a trip right now, and he stuffed his suitcase full of running shoes and jogging clothes. I couldn't fucking believe it. Old people have so much energy. My ankles hurt just thinking about it. But with the device, no more need for running.'

'Older folks are amazing. They've got so much energy, so much stamina. They go to work every day, and somehow they still find it in them to have love affairs. My mum had a steady stream of them until recently. Her ex-husband had a wife and four kids, and she was actually envious! It drove her crazy. And Daddy's second wife . . .'

Which made me remember. *HIS* pipsqueak girlfriend. Were they still engaged? Were they going to get married? I was intensely jealous now – just like our parents' generation would be. I had never known an emotion like it before. Is envy always the last emotion standing? (Things like respect and awe are long since gone. Everyone lives in a happy-go-lucky depression – they only take life half-seriously, you might say.)

'What's wrong?'

'Your girlfriend . . .'

'Oh yeah, I was about to tell you. *That's all set!*'

'I heard you were seeing her again.'

'I am. Just to talk. She went and got herself pregnant.'

'At the hospital? Were you the donor?'

'No, no, no. She went *natural*.'

'Gross.'

'It's a quirk of her metabolism. I couldn't believe it at first, but I guess it's true. She's no liar. That much I know.'

I lie all the time. I talk all kinds of bullshit. Something black began to stir deep inside me. 'But . . . this happened because of you?'

'She says she only dates one person at a time,' *HE* said, dodging my question. 'She says her head gets filled up with thoughts of that person, and here's the thing, she trusts me completely. She says things like, "You're a *good person*," and "I'll never betray you," and "We'll be together forever."'

'Bullshit. You're making this up.'

'I told you, didn't I? I mean, I seriously wonder if she's an angel or something. Her vitality, the force of her sexual desire. I don't think she would die even if you killed her. So I want to try it to find out.'

213

'I'm hanging up.'

My head hurt. I wanted to get into bed.

'Wait. I don't want a kid. I want to slip quietly into oblivion, all by myself. I have to do something about her. Help me.'

'If you're going to talk her out of it, do it on your own.'

'I'm no match for her, physically. Listen, please, can you come over today? Right now? I'm begging you.'

The screen flared to life, and I could see that HE was kneeling with HIS forehead pressed to the ground.

'Please, say something. I love you, for starters. You're my angel – no, my devil, my lovely devil. I mean it.'

HIS (father's) apartment was fully mechanized. Everything spick and span.

'This way.'

HIS room was especially clean, airy and pleasant. Seemed like a nice place to spend your time. A video camera was set up in one corner.

'What do you record?'

'My daily life.'

'And you watch it later? Wow, must be riveting.'

'Sometimes.' HE adjusted the lighting, temperature, and fan.

'You clean a lot, huh.'

'It passes the time.' HE put on a tape. It showed the square near the Koma Theater. 'It's from that day. I got the guy to make me a copy.'

The murder played out again on screen.

'Doesn't have much impact, does it.'

'Right? If I don't keep reminding myself that "this really happened," it seems so lacklustre. But the angle's bad and the camera shakes, so it's really not like a TV show either. This has been copied so many times, see how the picture quality's degraded? Makes it feel so much more authentic.'

'The parts you can't see all that clearly stimulate the imagination.'

'Exactly. Now this I bought the other day. It's a document of someone's suicide. Apparently the guy was up to his ears in debt, and he made this so his family could sell it and pay off the loans. And it was a hit. Want to see?' HE switched out the tape.

A sober-looking middle-aged man was making introductory remarks. He was about the same age as my father (hadn't Dad committed suicide!) and they looked pretty similar, but of course it wasn't him.

'He sounds so matter-of-fact.'

'Right? Makes it seem so real.'

The man on the screen said, 'OK, here we go,' then drank something that must've been poison from a bottle.

'What is that?'

'He was trying to be so meticulous, but he forgot to say. Now *that's* truth.'

Even in this day and age, we still revere truth. But at the same time, we devote ourselves to the task of erasing the distinction between truth and fiction.

'Is it fertilizer?' It was a serious question, but HE apparently took it as a joke since the man didn't look anything at all like an agricultural worker. 'I never knew you had such a cruel streak.'

'I like to keep you on your toes. Ah, to be Terence Stamp,' HE said coquettishly.

'Who?'

'Come on, *The Collector*.'

'Of what?'

'It's a movie. He plays this amaaazing guy. By the way . . .'

HE searched my face. I looked away, and when I looked back HE was still staring at me. I had a sudden premonition and crossed my arms in front of me. 'No, don't kill me!'

A faint smile touched HIS lips.

'. . . Not you,' HE crooned. 'You're not pregnant. She's on her way here.'

'But, that's . . .'

'I can't do it alone. It would be too exhausting. I need you to hold her down, since I'm sure she'll fight back.'

'I don't want to.'

'I think it'll be simplicity itself once we actually get going. Wringing her neck or whatever.'

'If I were the pregnant one, would it be the other way around? Would you get her to help kill me?'

'Probably, yeah. But so what? Think of it as a TV show. Pretend you're an actor.'

'I don't think I can get myself into that headspace.'

'I'm going to tape it, too.'

What the hell is HE thinking?

HE took both of my hands in HIS and sat down. 'Once it's over, it'll be like nothing even happened. You can't hide your sadistic side from me. And didn't you tell me that when you were a kid, your mother tried to kill you a couple of times? Like Mary Bell.'

'I have no intention of helping you.'

'This really happened, in England: Two girls, eleven and thirteen, killed a three-year-old boy and a four-year-old boy, but the eleven-year-old was smarter and cleverer, and the older girl was just following her lead. She was acquitted, but the eleven-year-old was convicted.'

'I don't want to hear about it.'

'Then, what about Lizzie Borden?'

'Stop it. What are you getting at?'

'That the way you yourself were raised was problematic. An endless cycle of absurd coddling and other horrible experiences, right?'

'You *your*self, why are you—'

'Don't be stupid. There'll be one more *good* tape in the world! And, if it comes out and I get caught, the police will track down my mum for me, I'm sure of it.'

The doorbell rang.

Around dawn I became hysterical, and my crying woke HIM. It felt like the first time I had cried in my whole life. HE patted my hand gently to try and calm me down.

'There's nothing to worry about. Tomorrow you'll go and get the surgery. The one to get the electrode installed in your brain. Then you can relax forever.'

I tugged as hard as I could at the end of my stocking. HE had lit the flame of my envy. Her corpse was crammed into the freezer. Eyes closed, tongue lolling out.

'What'll we do now?'

'Get married.'

'No thanks. Who wants to share this kind of memory?'

'Under the current law, testimony from a spouse is inadmissible. So it'd be better for both of us if we got married. Like in *Brighton Rock*.'

How can HE be so calm? Is it because of the device?

'Wanna do it? It's been a long time.'

'Do what? Oh . . . But the sheets might get dirty.'

I didn't want to be in the room where we'd killed her, so we were sleeping in HIS father's bed.

'It's fine.'

HE took me in HIS arms. I just lay there the whole time, worrying about the sheets.

When it was over, HE opened HIS eyes, and seemed to be seeing something else.

The boredom is gone.